I0587495

Charles Conrad Abbott

Clear Skies and Cloudy

Charles Conrad Abbott

Clear Skies and Cloudy

ISBN/EAN: 9783337349349

Printed in Europe, USA, Canada, Australia, Japan

Cover: Foto ©Andreas Hilbeck / pixelio.de

More available books at **www.hansebooks.com**

CLEAR SKIES AND CLOUDY

BY
CHARLES C. ABBOTT, M.D.

PHILADELPHIA & LONDON
J. B. LIPPINCOTT COMPANY
MDCCCXCIX

To the

Amateur Naturalists

and to whomsoever loves an outing, and to

every Audubon Society in these

United States,

these desultory papers on

subjects closely akin to their aims and pleasures

are respectfully dedicated

by

The Author

Three Beeches, January 12, 1898

Preface.

HE who keeps even so simple a matter as a record of the weather will find that the years are not very much alike. At this writing there is that contradiction, a warm east rain prevailing, although mid-January, and a year ago, this date, it was clear and cold; and so with practically every feature of Nature, comparing the days of one year with another. The rambler finds that history does not repeat itself, except where the principal phenomena are grouped. Birds nest in May and June and migrants come and go at about the same time, but the success of some outing that is vividly remembered is not likely to be repeated when you go again on the morning of your red-letter day to the same upland field, deep, dark wood, or open, sunny meadow. Would it be well if it were so? There is more merit in uncertainty than satisfaction in foreknowledge. The latter smacks of omniscience as derisively applied to humanity, and such unfortunates are apt to bore us.

To foresee the flowers and forehear the birds might be sufficiently satisfactory, if you are lazily inclined, and so the suggested outing foredone, which means staying in-doors and doing nothing. The ever-present possibility of novelty is an incentive that should prove all-powerful, and nowhere is the world so worn out that the unexpected may not happen. What of the showers of frogs, fish, and worms of which we sometimes read? To be caught in such a shower, and without an umbrella too, would probably stir up the dormant instincts that make us all curious as to Nature in her playful moods. It ought to, if it does not.

It was not long ago that a distinguished archæologist came to this neighborhood to see the indubitable evidences of man's antiquity that had recently been unearthed. He came late in the day, but in time to see what was to me of much greater interest, a superb sunset. His attention was called to it, but he replied with a groan, and not looking up even, as he spoke, "I have not had my dinner. Can't the sunset wait?"

One of the few facts about which there can be no disputing is, that Nature will not wait for us : to secure her favor we must do the waiting. I was not surprised, however, at the remark made by the hungry savant, for there never was so enthusiastic a nature-lover yet that at times his stomach did not rule his head and heart ; but enthusiasm should be pitched to such a key that we, at least, prefer suffering under clear skies rather than cloudy. Without a willingness to suffer in some slight degree, the rambler makes little progress in instructive observation. The best of what is out of doors is not always at arm's length. Healthy enthusiasm is a rational phase of the spirit of adventure, but adventure does not necessarily mean distance, be it understood. The dimly outlined forest that you people with many novelties too often proves a tamer wood-lot than your own back yard.

It has been suggested that "the loathsome and the dangerous in nature" should be slurred over on account of the readers' prejudices, which are intensified and not set aright by the author telling the plain truth. The rambler and the author should always remain as widely apart as the poles. Certainly—not merely probably or possibly, but certainly—the rambler so far unfits himself to ramble if he has at the outset the subsequent *rôle* of authorship in mind. This is evident if we give the subject a moment of calm consideration. What will go to the making of the liveliest essay? is the inevitable question, and deciding upon some sure-to-be-seen bird or flower, you face but blurred images of everything save the selected flower or bird. Literally, you have been walking and actually seen some object of more or less interest, but this is far removed from a genuine ramble, when you live up to the golden rule of equal consideration for all. The essay is written, but is it not unfair to the central object? Why not overcome our prejudices and accept the world as it is? To take our most gorgeous beetle from his chosen home and set him upon a rose-bud may suit the delicate nerves of my lady fair, but what of Nature? Are we to say outright that Nature is indelicate, lacks taste, and is all unworthy of entrance into the courts of the refined? Out upon such rot ! Have you seen your bird and flower as it really is when you have seen nothing but it? That which led to it, and all that filled the world when it itself passed from view, had some bearing upon it which you have missed. If to reach some desired bird or flower you have to pass through a den of snakes, do so, and if moved to tell your story, say so. Do not slur over snakes for sake of any supposed objection to them. Serpents are as much a part of Nature as any flower of hill or dale. I never heard more exhilarating songs than those of the Carolina wren, that stays all day in the barn-yard and roosts, for aught I know, in the pig-pen ; and I do not propose to transplant that bird to the flower-garden or set it up on the lawn to slur over the prosaic truth.

Having rambled as Nature's guest, do not be mean enough to misrepresent her. The "loathsome and dangerous" must not be over-looked if the author is true to her, and loyalty there, rather than to people's prejudices, should be his ambition. If seen aright, Nature is never loathsome; it is only the unhealthy human being that is excited to nausea and disgust, as the dictionary puts it, by Nature, whatsoever the form she takes or work she performs. To slur certain phases of natural operations over is simply to be a coward, and no author but should care infinitely more about himself than about his readers. The author is not his brother's keeper to such an extent that he must neglect himself.

This is a tempting subject, but I forbear. My little day has been spent with few people, and usually with none at all. Possibly I am all wrong,—certainly I do not care; but will remain happy until I can no longer see a sunset or hear a song-sparrow.

It may interest the reader to know that the accompanying illustrations were all taken by or for the author, and are points of view at his own home, or just over the boundary, on the lands of his neighbors.

C. C. A.

THREE BEECHES, June 2, 1898.

Contents.

List of Illustrations.

Frost Foliage.

A WONDER-WORKER is this elfish frost. He deals not only in fantastic shapes, but crowds the fields in a single night with glittering, crystalline ghosts of dead summer's blossoms. At daybreak they tremble in the restless wind and tearfully stand their ground at sunrise. Their master, arrant coward, has hidden in the shadows. The rising sun breaks the spell and the ghosts are gone.

Emboldened by the north wind, it sometimes happens that frost works with greater vigor through the watches of the night, and then there are not only the same dainty blossoms as before, but the skeletons of the frail growths of summer are rebuilt in crystal ;— firmly rebuilt, and so rugged that the sun's level rays only add to their splendor, and for half a day, the fields are prismatic instead of brown, and so brilliant that all we recall of summer's best efforts seem crude and merely gaudy, never grand.

Frost is crowned king when autumn wears away, and then the poetry of his early efforts, when a petty prince, gives place to sturdy building that defies the jealous sun.   Even the

river yields to his command, and we have an after-taste of the time when arctic conditions prevailed and men who wandered in this river valley were held back by a mighty glacier. Long ago, but not all trace of it has vanished.

Even the finger-marks of man have not been erased. Likewise, too, every babbling brook and rippling creek is silent in his presence.

Given the water turned to rock, the ground covered with snow and moonlight,—these together,—and we have that "all silence and all glisten" that Lowell used as a background to a charming in-door scene ; but what of this background itself, and more particularly when there is sound instead of silence, and sunlight instead of pallid moonshine? The air to-day was full of frozen mist, invisible needle-points, that pricked the skin and played painful pranks with the ears of pedestrians ; but, putting aside such minor inconveniences as this, can we put on a real winter change and be as much one with Nature now as in summer? It is a question I have often asked, and if the columns of answers were added up, I fear the result would show that one pedestrian at least is a tropical animal. There is a greater effort needed now to meet Nature's requirements. More clothing, more food, and artificial heat, if we halt upon our journey ; but are we not repaid? Can the result be looked upon with doubt when we sum up the joys of a winter camp-fire? I do not mean a blazing roar of consuming logs and a crowd about it,—from such defend me,—but in some sheltered nook to kindle a few gathered twigs, and, absorbing all the heat, come in closest contact with Nature in the days of frostiness.

I could see through the thick ice that the brook was flowing still, and if it could wait in patience for the coming of spring why not I? To-day it looked through icy windows and was content, while I was free. The leaping flames crackled merrily and the sand beneath them began to flow. I had made the spot a little tropic for the time, and how quickly word was passed and my neighbors came to see! There was the hum of a town's activity down every twiggy avenue, and the airy lines of travel, long deserted, were alive again, as the snow-birds and tree-sparrows came trooping hither, and all because a weary pedestrian had built a little fire and was resting himself. It is well that birds do not carry thermometers or study the paths of storms, and, man-like, anticipate all possible discomforts. The mercury sank to four degrees in the night, but the birds' spirits did not sink in proportion. Winter is outside of their feathers and there it is welcome. If it steals their food, the birds laugh at their ill luck and steal a march on winter. A few wing-beats and the matter is mended. Who cares? is the theme of every one of them, and man, muffled in furs and shivering over a fire, calls himself the lord of creation. So he is, but until he is as independent as the birds there is one spoke lacking to perfect his wheel.

My little camp-fire was a new world to me, and, as it seemed, a new world to the friends that flocked about me. Here came the two nuthatches and the brown creeper; the Carolina wren and the winter wren from northward; the golden-crowned kinglet and tree-sparrows; the chickadee and his crested cousin, and, as if to overlook them and warn of my hostile intentions, if I had any, came two chattering jays. I sat still for a while, and every one of these birds seemed to enjoy a smoke-bath. The curling, thread-like cloud no sooner reached the lower branches of the trees than the birds flitted through it, and then chattered in great glee as they came to rest on the brittle twigs of the shrubbery. I sat still, and drinking in the warmth made no motion but with my eyes. Not a bird but came closer, and as I measured after, many were within three feet of my face. Only the jays held moderately aloof, and probably by so doing showed to a greater advantage. After all, is there not much in wildness that is to be commended? If birds flew in our open windows and perched like flies on our bald heads during a summer nap, then our interest might flag. It is possible to maintain an interest in things we cannot touch and to lose interest in them when too often in our hands. The jays, by reason of their size and brilliant plumage, made fitting background to the winsome wee birds that desired to fathom the mystery of my fire. But what has all this to do with frost foliage? Nothing, perhaps, to you, even after my explanation, but much to me. Not a bird in the bush or on a tree but is a winter bird; a bird as characteristic of this January day as are the swallows of summer sunshine. They have come, as it were, to me to replace the leaves. They revivify the landscape, and, coming at the call of frost, I associate them with his crystalline lifeless handiwork. Frost-work, in all its infinite variety, is a fitting accompaniment to feathers in their complexity. We have since the beginning of time associated birds and blossoms, and to many it may seem a novelty to have the one without the other. But Nature is not partial; the summer songsters have not all of the world's glories to themselves. My brave winter wren and tits and nuthatches brave the frost foliage, and when they sport among it the glory of winter sunshine is apparent.

My little wayside camp-fire is but a heap of ashes; the smoke that arose from it has drifted miles. The birds that gathered, one by one, as I tarried, have left me; and now I, too, pass to other points, to a meadow here, a field there, and through the dark cedars that fringe a highway, and wherever I turn there is no repulsive nakedness,—the trees, the shrubs, the very skeletons of the dead grasses, are made beautiful again, clothed in frost foliage.

An Ice-Bound Brook.

IT is a genuine comfort to know the nature of our footing; to be rid of doubt when we walk. The possible near presence of a quicksand perturbs the mind until we are dead to Nature's attractions. Sometimes, however, such a doleful experience is repaid by the ecstatic reaction when firm earth is reached, after treading some treacherous path. We laugh at the very idea of having entertained a fear and grow bolder as the distance increases between danger and ourselves.

Often, throughout the long summer and dreamy autumn-tide, I had wandered as near as prudence permitted to the wide brook that flowed silently and swiftly through the weedy marsh, but never quite reached to those river sanctuaries that held, in fact or in fancy, the chief glories of these unreclaimed tracts of meadow. But kindly frost came to my aid.

Through the long watches of one starry night, when not a twig of the tall, sentinel trees trembled, so gentle was the passing breeze, the current was stayed in its haste, and before the sun rose there was no rippled surface of flowing water, but in its place a path of crystal.   Firm ice, blue-black and clear as glass, from bank to bank, but not down to the very bed of the shallow stream ; a covering that made the channel accessible and possible to observe beyond any means that I could have devised.   And so I have been spending ideal hours in an ideal spot.

Not all the green growths that, when summer was most active, almost stopped the current of the brook are wilted and wasted by the touch of frost.   There is a green and growing mat of ribbon-like and hair-like plant life in the bed of the stream that forever waves and trembles, but not wholly because the water is in constant motion.   Look long and steadily through the clear ice, and at times you will be rewarded by seeing sudden movements of dark objects, a sudden darting here and there of living creatures, that, if thought of at all, you supposed were taking a winter-long nap deep down in the mud. These many objects are not disturbed by some unusual occurrence and your presence has nothing to do with it. Aquatic life, in part, hibernates, sleeping as soundly as any jumping mouse on land, but it does not take any fish or turtle so long to wake up, and some of these creatures sleep with one eye open. This is quite evident when a musk-rat goes fumbling down the ditch, poking its nose into everybody's business, if one may judge from its actions. Stupid suckers, our most ungainly fish, except when young, hurry in their awkward way from the matted grass in which they were resting; a pike, our most graceful fish, will dart like an arrow and as suddenly disappear; and that sleepy-looking, but not fool of a fish, the mud minnow, will be neither sluggish nor precipitant, but duly methodical, and effectually dodge any real or suspected danger. The musk-rat means no harm. Its journey down Water street, as we might call it, is a peaceful errand; but wild life, whether in the water or in the air above it, is not given to running unnecessary risks. Perhaps a musk-rat might feel carnivorously inclined, and a bite by his jaws wounds no less surely and severely than a nip from an otter or a mink. Explain it all as we may, there is a commotion under the ice through which we look, and we forget the stagnation of the surrounding meadows that lie all uncomfortably cold in the clear but unreviving sunshine of January.

At this moment I hear the trill of song-sparrows at intervals, but here, to my fancy, is something even better, wild life seen without long waiting between the acts. Only a few small fishes, it is true, but where in any museum or library shall we go to learn that which we would like to know of these few fish? The learned ichthyologist is wholly concerned with the creatures' bones and scales; the angler passes them by contemptuously; the amateur naturalist fears to draw too near lest he wets his feet, or must come only on some sunny summer day. It is a pity it is so. There is more to be seen in a weedy, ice-bound brook in January than my neighbor fancies. The little pike, sucker, sunfish, and many a so-called minnow is now neither dead nor sleeping, but ready at a moment's notice to play, as I am moved to call it, with the fishes nearest by ; or the larger ones to indulge in the more serious sport of swallowing the little fellows within their reach, exhibiting here a perfect counterpart of one phase of human activities.

To find fish within fish, even three or four, "telescoped," as it were, big, smaller, little, and wee fish—all this is no uncommon occurrence. But to go into particulars makes the whole subject appear ridiculous.   I saw lately a fish which reminded me of a pocket spy-glass, short and stout ; but when fish after fish was revealed and placed in a row, then it was like this same spy-glass drawn out until every section was exposed. In this case it was a matter of three fishes,—a pike, a mud-minnow, and a very small pike. Equally ravenous at times is the black pirate perch.   Tales of horror might be told of the ceaseless warfare that goes on, summer and winter, even in such little brooks as this in the meadow.   A few days of unusual warmth reaches down a few inches into the mud and turtles will stretch themselves.   The larger predatory fishes regain their appetites, and terror reigns in the camps of the minnows. The grasses and pendulous growths that now so peacefully wave with the gentle current may at any moment be tossed tumultuously aside, and the water be roiled for a rod or more of its present crystalline course. It is not always a

pike that is at the bottom of the mischief. A mink may surprise the pike, that is at the moment premeditating murder, and for an instant pandemonium reigns.

My little brook is but a mere remnant now of the pretentious stream of other days ; and,

with its loss of volume, there has been un-
happily a loss of wild life which formerly found
the world here Nature at her best. Otters are
all gone, I suppose. The last pair, it may
be, were those killed within a few months.
The beaver has been long extinct, but, while
no trace of a dam remains, the bones of these
creatures are common in the ashes of Indian
cooking sites. Even the lumpish, lazy musk-
rats have a host of enemies forever at their
heels. Think of those to come after us, re-
duced to the contemplation of meadow mice.
I am almost too late, but the savage within me
pleasantly thrills my breast as I make out the
frozen tracks of a raccoon, now firm in texture
as fossil footprints. It is useless to follow them
up, but there is some satisfaction, upon their
basis, of repeopling the brookside. Even now,
sitting at the foot of a cluster of silvery birches,
I can see not only the coon, but its more formidable cousin, the bear. Not strange, this,
for I saw only yesterday a bear's tooth, picked
from an upland field, which some Indian had
worn as an ornament. Is not this the secret of
the satisfaction we sometimes have in wander-

ing about? Not so much what a thing is as what it suggests, I take it, as the secret of that content that eases weary limbs when we have walked for miles. To wander by this brook-side now, intent only on its ice, its mossy banks, and the leafless trees that skirt its winding course; intent, I say, only on these as they are individually, is "to feel like one who treads alone some banquet hall deserted." The plain truth of the matter is, there now are no living creatures to be seen or heard, and frozen ground, thinly carpeted with dead grass, does not exhilarate like the rank growths of summer. It is too cold, too, to speculate, and why at such a time are winter birds so unreasonable? All things are favorable, from my point of view, yet not a bird will show itself, and the song-sparrows no longer sing, even fitfully. The silence of a winter day is maddening, and were it not that we have just expectations of at least one chickadee, the rambler had better stay at home; but I hear jays now in the hill-side beeches and quarrelling crows along the frozen river. Such sounds bring content. A lively activity that defies the cold is assuring, and the little brook is at once a braver feature of the landscape. I have often wondered why winter landscapes are more popular on canvas than in real life. Strange misconceptions of the world in winter are everywhere prevalent. The winter sunrise has a more brilliant array of colors than a summer sunset, and winter sunsets lose much by being seen through a window. The clearer air, the snowy foreground, the interlacing of leafless branches, through which we look, all add their mite to the glory of the close of day. And when, at last, as you turn your steps homeward, you hear a song-sparrow trill lightly as it is perched on the frozen twig, and perhaps see it firmly outlined against an illuminated background, as I did to-day, you will feel that to trace the meadow brook, though icy-cold the air, is not merely to brave the rigors of winter, but to be one with earnest life that can teach us many a useful lesson, if so be we are willing to be taught.

Winter Bells.

THE winter bells ring merrily to-day. In the glittering sunshine the gathered tree-sparrows chirped and twittered their childish hymn to Peace. Bright and beautiful the day, without a moment of depressing silence. Lisping chickadees came near to where I sat, not listening to them, as perhaps they thought, but to the ringing, clear and sharp, of the winter bells. They were ringing out their delight, not "in the icy air of night," but in the crystalline atmosphere of a February noon. We are too apt, at such a time, to spend our energy in searching out the signs of Spring, and so remain unmindful of the day's peculiar merits. Shrug your shoulders, if you will, and turn contemptuously away, but February has something to be said in its favor.

Here I am in a remote, weed-grown, long neglected meadow ; home of more wildness and strange fruits of Nature's fancy than any other spot to be reached in a day's ramble; alone, and likely to be so unless I meet with some old trapper or, less probable, wandering freak as aimless as myself.   But I have not come in vain; the winter bells are ringing.   They ring to call the sunbeams to this pretty spot, ring

for the birds that now are gathering here, ring, I wish I dared to think it, for me too to come and share in the general joy of this February noon.

Welcome or not, none order me away, and I am urged to tarry because of no offensive demonstration. He who would know the joy of an outing, whether in midwinter or during the long and languid summer days, must have evidence such as mine of a wild bird's confidence. Thoreau's wood-chopper liked to have the chickadees about him. Little wonder that he did, for now while I am listening to the tinkling of merry winter bells, these birds come near; so near they look me directly in the face and chirp, in a quizzical way, *You here?* Nothing more delightful than this in any welcome among people in town. Yes, I am here, and the bells ring on as sweetly as ever; never tiring of their own sweet music, nor can I ever, I feel, grow weary of listening. Winter is but an empty word to-day; the cold gray clouds suggest no chilling thoughts; little it matters that the branches of the trees are bare;—the winter bells are ringing!

I hear the wrangling crows, so like mankind in all their disagreeable ways, where they have gathered along and on the river, and I can see them, in my mind, wandering about that desolate scene, floating on the huge ice-rafts, scrambling for stray bits brought by the recent flood, and hovering over the blue-black waters, as fancy pictures foul spirits in a gloomier world, but nothing of all this reaches here. The trees, the earth, the very air itself, strain out all harshness from the crows' ill-natured cries, and only that which is pleasing is heard where the winter bells are ringing.

I hear the rapid blows upon some dead tree on the hill-side, and I know that the woodpecker is at work, or is it merely noisy sport to him? The sound brings out to me in bold relief the lonely remnant of the ancient forest, bleak and bare and silent now, save for this bold bird that wakes the echoes, it may be, to keep his courage up. Winter means everything there that we would shun ; the very mosses crack like brittle glass, and no creature ventures now to wander over the wood-path's carpet of crisp autumn leaves. Not a sunbeam turns aside to cheer the woods ; they have other things to do, and, choosing gayety to sorrow, linger content where winter bells are ringing.

I hear a rustling in the dead grass near me. Soon the gaunt, frail skeletons of a summer's growth are ruthlessly turned aside, and close to where I sit a musk-rat pauses and stares at me with evident fear, yet not to the exclusion of astonishment. *You here?* he seems to ask, and seeing that I make no movement, a trace of confidence is his, and he turns towards the bells as if the more intently to listen to their music. I feel that I must laugh aloud, and do so, and in an instant my furry friend is gone. Gone, too, was every chickadee and the song-sparrow that had sung in dulcet tones, perched in a mossy nook above the bells. I could hear, for the time, neither crows nor the woodpecker. Our birds are steadily learning a good deal; have already learned to their sorrow what mankind usually proves to be to them, but never have they rightfully interpreted laughter. Crows laugh, in spite of what the bumptious professionals may say, and parrots have a keen sense of humor; but it is wisdom on the part of the rambler not to express himself in such a way when amused by what he sees. Human laughter would be to us a harsh, repelling sound if we did not realize its significance, and we know all too well it often means mischief and not merriment. Like a fool, I laughed, and in an instant the spot where I lingered was well-nigh robbed of all its charms ; would quite have been had not, happily, the winter bells kept ringing.

Only very slowly is confidence restored in the breasts of wild life. It seemed a long time before I could hear the chirp of any returning bird, and the winter bells tolled rather than rang out merrily. But the birds did come again. Chickadees, tree-sparrows, the brown creeper, and a nuthatch came and chatted pleasantly among themselves or to themselves ; it matters not which. Enough that I heard them and that they had forgotten my awkward blunder of laughing aloud. Very different in their ways, these birds, and the variety added interest to the outlook, and again the winter bells struck a livelier note and rang out so cheerfully, no one worried about the time of year. Winter all over the world, for aught we care, but nothing of its dulness lingers here when the winter bells are ringing.

To know what the out-door world fully means, we must enter into the spirit of the scenes, must be enthusiastic, and then it is not impossible to divine the feelings of the birds that enliven such a place as this. You may come here and, after one swift glance, mutter "weeds and water," and go away, having spoken the simple, sober truth; true as when you say of a city, "bricks and mortar." Having but his flesh and bones before you, can you say, "here is a man"? Literally true of where I am at present, weeds and water, but if forced to seat yourself at the foot of a tree and hold a weed before your eyes; to count its joints and branches; to note each frost crystal that clings to it;—you will likewise be forced to admit that a weed in winter is not merely decaying vegetation. Its summer freshness may be gone, but its winter suggestiveness remains until summer comes again and appeals as strongly to those who love Nature not as she is at times, but as she is always, and can fairly shout for joy when the bright sunshine holds all shadows back and winter bells are ringing.

If obstinate to the point of seeing no beauty in a weed, may not water hold you a moment? It is not always as terrifying as the ocean in a storm or lifeless as in a muddy mill-pond. Here is something akin to neither extreme,—a sparkling rivulet that has worn its winding way through the meadows to the river, where it adds its mite to the greater stream and is lost in the ocean at last. We need not trace it throughout so long a journey. Here it is the prattling infant rather than a staid old man, an artless child rather than a cunning adult,—a rivulet, born of the spring that lives in some underground recess, and he who loves an outing cannot see and hear it unimpressed. As I see it now, this laughing brook looks up for a moment at the blazing sun and then darts behind the ice-bound masses of old leaves that have lodged by its way; then, turning and twisting among the airy roots of an old elm, swirls about the domed house of a musk-rat, and then in and out among the hassocks of the open meadow. It is silent at one point, tuneful at another, but never sober and downcast. Its lively spirit moves or ought to move you. Its presence alone means beauty and joy, and means even more now and here, at this passing moment, when many a bird is singing its praises and the winter bells are ringing.

The sunny day is waxing old apace. An envious shadow is creeping hitherward, and already its repressing influence is felt. The bells are ringing in a more deliberate way. One by one the sparrows fly farther and farther afield, seeking new regions where the sun still brightly shines; the chickadees have wandered to the woods again, where now the sunlight falls invitingly. The change here, where I have been these hours, is felt rather than seen, and my curiosity is piqued. I tarry yet longer, until silence reigns supreme. Not a bell but now is stilled and hints no more of music than the solemn birch-trees that tower far above them.

I have not proved as fitful as the birds; I have been more faithful than the wandering sun; but now the cords are snapped that bound me; the spirit of restlessness is strong again. I too hie me away to lovelier scenes, if happily I may find them; but what, I am asked on turning away, of these winter bells? True, I had almost forgotten. The icicles had ceased to drip, the sparkling water no longer fell, drop by drop, upon the ice below. These tiny spheres of music were now no longer free; no longer rang these charming winter bells.

A Corvine Congress.

ABOVE the roar of the petulant east wind that bent the tops of the pines about the house, whistled through the big door-yard elm and passed over the meadows, twisting and twirling twigs and dead leaves in its path,—above all this I heard the clamor of many crows that had congregated in the white-oak grove near the mouth of the gully through which hurries an upland brook on its way to the river. I heard these crows better than I could see them, so, armed with a field-glass, I cautiously approached their meeting site by a circuitous route, and happily escaped discovery by any one of the several sentinels that were most judiciously posted at all points of approach that might prove dangerous. The grove where this particular session of congress was held is well adapted for the purpose on such a day as this, being sheltered from the east wind, except about the tops of the tallest trees; a rural coliseum, fit for all avian exhibitions, and never quite forsaken, the round year, either by night or day. But perhaps I had better refrain from even the very plainest, least varnished account of what I saw and heard. The cry of imagi-

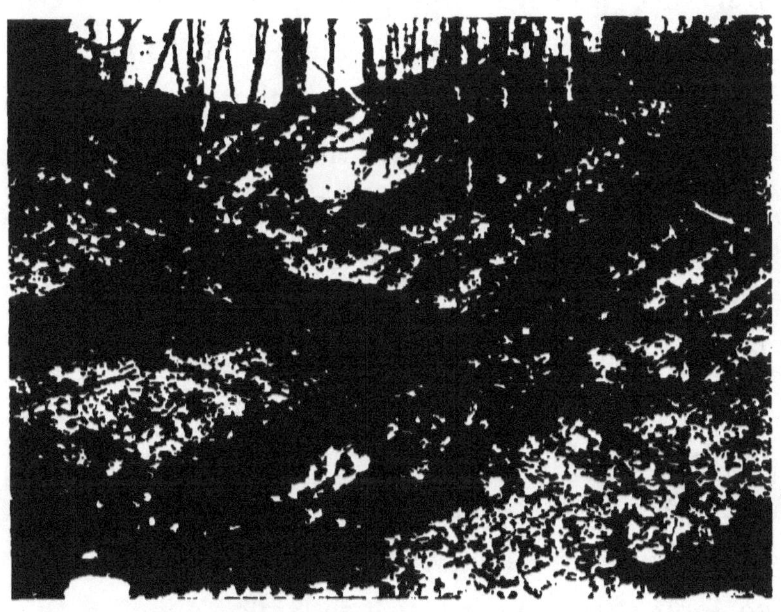

nation run wild, of investing birds with attributes not belonging to creatures lower than men, and all that ultra-scientific rubbish of theorists,—all this is so vehemently proclaimed when a courier arrives from the woods, that one may well question if a personal narrative of out-door incidents is worth the while to print. It is true, an ever increasing interest in a particular species of bird may make us a bit careless as to painfully extreme accuracy, our enthusiasm making every act and utterance of rather more significance than the facts warrant, but this, however much it is to be deplored, is less undesirable than the cold-blooded announcement of the anatomist that a crow flies and screams "caw" at all times and is as black as the ace of spades. This is true, but is it quite all of corvine ornithology? No one doubts the cunning of a fox, and a crow is a fox in feathers. It is the most intelligent of all our birds, and I do not suppose any one doubts that there is a great difference among our birds as to their mental calibre. Perhaps it is doubted. The world has groped in error so long that now it loves the false even to the point of idolatry, and truth is offered no kindly welcome when it timidly appears. I am not an omnivorous reader of books, and so speak only for myself. I have gathered from first hands—that is, from the birds themselves—that some are quick-witted, others foolish, and occasionally some are downright fools. You can hoodwink a wood-thrush, but it is a smart man that deceives a cat-bird, and never the second time. English sparrows know a trap however natural its appearance, and know my gun as something very different from a walking-stick. The peewee is confiding, but its big, yawping country cousin down the lane among the apple-trees, the great crest, is always suspicious. The chippy that nested by the parlor window took crumbs from my fingers ; but the humming-bird dashed at my eyes when I drew too near its nest. I never saw a chickadee that was not distinctly friendly ; but the crested tit says there is elbow-room enough for both it and myself, and demands so much neutral territory between us. The lines can be more closely drawn. There is marked difference among in-dividuals of the same species. You do not get at this from a chance acquaintance, meeting birds to-day and never afterwards. Circum-stances must bring you together and keep you associated for a season, and then, after such an experience, the whole world will appear to you in a different light. To annoy birds will not occur to you and bird-murder be unthinkable.

But the crows: what of them? Luckily, I gained an advantageous point of view, after a deal of painful crawling through the weeds; and briers' thorns are sharper in January than at other times, or human flesh more sensitive. Adjusting the field-glass, I saw—not fancied I saw—that one crow, from a commanding position, was haranguing the assembled multitude. What I heard was one crow's voice that varied or rang the changes on the basic syllable *kaw* about as follows: *kă—ce', kă kaw! kaw'kă;* and then there was a babel of *kaw—ka-ā-ā,* that clearly expressed assent, an apparent "that's so" that was ludicrously like the chatter of congregated humanity when an orator stoops to their comprehension. After a momentary pause, the orator, as we will call the speaking crow, resumed his speech, and the variations of *kaw kă* were repeated, but with many sounds like *ĕ-ĕ* and a trill, as *ar-r-r-r.* The latter were always, I thought, uttered in a more rapid manner than what I have called the basic syllable, *kaw,* and certainly were accompanied with more gestures. Accurate description is impossible, words and actions were so rapid, but my impression would doubtless not have varied had the crow been more deliberate. The most striking feature of it all, however, was the dissent of the gathering on two occasions, that was as plainly marked as the previous assent had been. The utterance was wholly different and the accompanying gestures likewise varied. The twisting and turning of the head and neck was most pronounced,—a turning away, as it were, from the suggestion ; and there was also a decided wing movement I did not notice before, corresponding in some measure to the hand and arm movement among ourselves when excited to the point of being demonstrative.

I am not sure at what time of day the congress opened its session, but it lasted for just twelve minutes after I took up my position in the spectators' gallery, if the tangle of briers can be so called. Then occurred a break in the proceedings, for one of the out-posted sentinels was heard to call out, not unlike a turkey, but the cry ending in a prolonged *er-r-r-r.*

This caused a sudden closing of the orator's speech, or argument, or whatever it really was, and the assembled crows rose into the air, some thirty feet or more above the trees. I noticed, by mere chance, that the sentinels remained perched in the trees. After the lapse of probably three or four minutes, the circling and chattering crows resumed their places, and what was to me most curious of all, in practically the same way they were previously distributed, and one individual, I shall always think the same, took up his position, in a way suggestive of being Speaker of the house. There was a brief repetition of the proceedings as described, and then a shout or extra-loud call uttered by every bird. The sentinels left their posts, and joining their brethren of the congress, the whole gathering flew away in the same westerly direction.

Now, if we are merely to witness what birds do and refrain from contemplating their motives in so doing, the great charm of out-door ornithology is gone. It is not satisfying to say there was a lot of crows in the oaks of the gully this morning and they made a great noise. It is not for an instant to be held that crows caw merely to hear themselves break the silence. There is nothing in all they utter akin to music. It is not intended as such more than the squealing of a pig. The associated acts and general deportment of the crows clearly show they have other purposes than soothing their excited nerves with song. But how do we know this? It is difficult to satisfactorily reply, inasmuch as it has been claimed, whether with good reason or not, that it is not justifiable to judge the non-human by the human standard. This may be true, but I know of no other standard. When a lower animal does the same thing that we would do under like circumstances, it seems thoroughly logical to assume that the intention is the same in either case. When we see our legislatures in session or recall the pleasant days of youthful debating societies, the purpose of the gathering together of a number of individuals is recognized at once, and would be if we were deaf and could hear not a word that was spoken. It is safe to say that a dog, entering a church during service, would recognize that the officiating clergyman was speaking and

the audience listening.   So in the case of the
crows to-day ; one harangued and the others
listened and occasionally commented upon what
was said ; possibly applauded.   These birds
have not copied all this from man, but it has
come about in their case, as in ours, gradually.
They have learned the value of consultation, and
that the *pros* and *cons* of a proposition must be
duly considered.   Certainly this was done to-
day by the crows assembled in my hill-side oaks,
and to reach such a point of complex mentality
means advanced intelligence.   Those wonderful
instincts about which, when children, we heard
so much played no part in what I have called a
corvine congress.   Even the posting of sentinels is not instinctive, but the result of fore-
thought based upon experience.   Truly, crows
are cunning, but not merely from necessitated
exercise of caution, as is possibly true of a fox,
but cunning to the degree of planning what
under given circumstances it is best to do ; and
how, with a fair measure of safety, they can pit
their intelligence against that of man.   Some
mammals do this and a few birds, but I know
of none in this country that go so far in the

direction of consideration of cause and effect as does the crow.

It is useless perhaps to hope ever to be able to translate the crows' language and so learn what they are discussing, whether but two or three are gathered together or a great flock is addressed by some chosen leader, but the initial step having long ago been taken, that communication of ideas among the lower animals does take place, it is no over-reaching of reasonableness to recognize that the variations of *kaw* and *ka* are full of meaning to the birds to which they are addressed.

A careful study of corvine courtship would be profitable to those who care for the subject of animal intelligence. Their mentality shows then, I doubt not, as prominently as when the nest is deserted and life is a struggle for food more than aught else. The actions of wooers have too frequently been commented upon as simply so many silly antics and not having any deeper meaning, but we are not yet sufficiently versed in ornithological lore to deliver snap judgments. It is a common practice, but sin is not less sinful because of its prevalence.

Among smaller birds than crows, the difficulties lie in the fact that we cannot detect all the utterances ; and it would not be surprising, if it could be proved, that birds intentionally whisper "little nothings" to those nearest to them. That male birds sing to attract the attention of females is undeniable, but there are other expressions of their feelings and responses by the females that are usually overlooked. Only at rarest intervals can we witness a courtship throughout and see for ourselves that birds are not mere machines, soulless and unsentimental, moved by impulses mysterious to themselves. I have seen a male rose-breasted grosbeak bring food to its mate and then, when the latter had taken it, rapidly move its beak in a manner clearly showing it was uttering some sound, which was quite inaudible to me. I have seen the flicker stop his work of cutting out a new nesting-place, and sitting close by the side of his mate, the two chatted, may I say? about their mutual interests, and then he would resume his work of deepening the cavity in the tree. Great, at times, is the chatter when the great crested flycatcher enters the nest and tells his mate to go out and take an airing and he will keep house while she is gone. But significant as is all that we see among mated birds, and we see but a mere fraction of what we should to pose as interpreters, it is little in comparison to that which is constantly transpiring among the crows. They do not live in fancied security as is true of other birds ; they accept nothing through hopefulness, and have no faith in appearances. Everything with which they have to deal must be tested as best they can, and so they live a life of constant fear, such as mankind finds intolerable. A happy crow, from our point of view, is an impossible creature ; but nevertheless, when crows do have a moderate sense of security, and know that their sentinels are alert and trustworthy, they venture to make merry among themselves and are playfully inclined. See them, for instance, gathered on cakes of floating ice when the river breaks up ; see them pitch and turn in mid-air with almost swallow-like agility ; see them hobnobbing with the gulls and hear them laugh ! Perhaps this is a step too far, but it is a wide-spread fancy, one I first heard of from an old fisherman, and I have never been able to rid myself of the idea that he was right. It seems so rational an interpretation of their wild cries as they are playing about the river, for surely not all their time is now spent in searching for food. The true inwardness of all corvine ways is not yet within our reach ; but when they are assembled as I saw them to-day and discussion is conducted decently and in order, then it is that the intelligence of these birds stands out quite unmistakably.

After the Storm.

STEADILY, for many long hours, the rain poured down, coming in long unbroken streams from the low-lying clouds. The sleepy brook that had murmured itself almost to sleep, as it crossed the lane, and languidly crept through the dark ravine that shuts out the sunlit world for many a rod, at last was roused to unwonted energy, and rushed forward to find the meadows of which it had been dreaming meadows no longer, but a lovely lake. Hour after hour, still it rained, and never night more dreary and more dark. The ominous roar of the wind among the door-yard trees made me tremble for the safety of the three beeches near my house, nor was my mind at ease until the gray-streaked dawn announced not only the break of day but the passing of the storm. The upland fields were all intact; the hill-side trees had suffered no injury, but there were no meadows !   I found myself living on the banks of a new-born lake.

I cannot explain it, but the simple fact is all-sufficient, the spirit of exploration and of adventure takes strong hold upon me, when, after the storm, the activity of resuming more nor-

mal conditions is at its height.   The puffy winds, the swiftly passing cloud, the scream of a hawk, the cawing of crows, the harsh cry of sea-gulls, and the nervous whistling of larks and red-birds, even the excited twitter of passing sparrows, all tend to rouse again my youthful energy, and, reckless of lessened suppleness and strength, I hurry away, scarce noting where,— only away, away! Now, if ever, the blessed wildness that is in us comes to the surface, and he who has most of it is the happiest of men. I do not speak hastily, I think, when saying this. We are backward in all that makes man what he was meant to be, when the grip of artificiality has throttled all desire to breathe the air beyond a village street. We hear much of higher aims and of the superlatively superior one of another existence, but must it be followed by ignoring and making little of that upon which we now dwell? I decline to make the sacrifice. The sunshine of to-day, after the storm, is bright enough ; anything brighter would be blinding and painful, not enjoyable. It is January, but I am afloat, not frozen in, as if in the arctic regions, and how grand the glittering sunlight on this nameless lake! No novelty, to be sure, but a repeated experience of these past forty years and more, but history has never repeated itself; and as of old, I am all eagerness to see and hear. Leaves are too tender for rude January days, yet the sapling sassafras is as green as a June meadow, and how stately the rich foliage of the rhododendrons! but here the slender silvery birches are bare intricacies of delicate twigs, a pretty lace-work as seen against the sky, and even prettier now that a host of waxwings has settled among them. They lisp in a languid way and never cease to dress rebellious feathers, but they do not rouse our interest beyond their prettiness. They lack the animation of a wren and music of a thrush, and one wonders what their place in Nature really is. This is not an unusual time for them, but their coming and going is very uncertain. Not always, however, for I have known a flock of half a hundred or more to linger about the same cedars for weeks together.

Of greater interest than any strictly land bird are the gulls that the storm has driven up the river, veritable storm-tossed creatures that happily do not complain, but enter into the new conditions with abundant zest. They give a seaside twang to the air and water, and I fancy the wind in the trees the roar of the surf. Other sea-birds occasionally come, and a good many too, at times, were here, long ago, judging from their bones in the Indian kitchen-refuse heaps and old cooking sites. Hawks add wildness to the wintry sky, and a black falcon on the bare branch of some outstanding tree is of course the shining mark towards which persecuting crows impetuously dart.

I need not row. The wind carries the boat in that aimless way that is so desirable when bound for no harbor. There are no breakers ahead. I am due nowhere, answerable to no one. Free as the wind is free; aimless; in love, for the moment, with every new bird that comes; devoted follower of the wandering musk-rat; ardent admirer of the drowned-out mice; everything and all things unto each and every creature; torn from my moorings, like my neighbor's fence-rails; free and happy. The storm, while it lasted, produced no pain, but still there was a feeling of restraint. I could have stood out in it and there was no one to stay me, yet I was restrained. The gloomy night suggested nothing to make me love life or the world; but the day, the sunlit hours after the storm, mean everything, and to float on these joyous waters that meet the passing breezes half-way and cap their waves with foam,—this is life, the moments snatched from year-long drudgery, that are not to be forgotten.

Where in the long summer days I was wont to ramble on foot, seeking the cool shadows or hidden spring of cool and crystal-clear waters, now I go in a different fashion, and not a landmark deigns to greet me. These old trees have withdrawn their friendliness, and I am a stranger among them ; but I will not be rebuffed. There is no wind murmuring in their branches, but the breaking of waves against their sturdy trunks is no less musical. For a while it is more dreamland than reality, but I am called at last to facts that crowd all fancies to the wall. The flood has unsettled the purposes of the meadow wild life, and by chance I see that mice, a squirrel, and some ill-defined creature have taken refuge here. They do not make any effort to escape or elude detection, but sit in a philosophical way, waiting for a change in the surroundings ; but what interested me most was to see that when required creatures that live in one place can adapt themselves readily to another. I never saw a meadow mouse climb a tree, but here are three that must have climbed the perpendicular trunk of a maple for at least five feet, the distance between the water's surface and the lowest branch. Above them crouches some larger mammal, but what is it? It hides itself effectually, and I can form no idea from what little I see. Possibly a young raccoon ; less probably a "wild" domestic cat ; it is too dark for an opossum, and skunks cannot climb, it is said. It is not strange to find the freshets upsetting wild life's plans ; even the moles in the upland fields have been burrowing in every direction, and uplifted the sod near the house into long disfiguring ridges.

All day long afloat and never tiring, though no adventure awaits me. As noon approaches the sun shines with unusual warmth, and my neighbor's bees come from the hive. There are insects in the air on the sunny sides of the oaks and hickories. How very quick to respond to a little sunshine is nearly every form of life ! and how very apt to suffer because of this credulity ! The winter sun, with us, can lie in a most unblushing manner. To-morrow, the mercury may sink to zero,—a drop of fifty-five degrees. I have known still greater changes. The only uniformity I have ever found is at Nine Spring Corner, where the water is always warm, plant-life luxuriant, and pretty salamanders always to be found.

If there was no adventure awaiting me, there was something equally good, a splendid sunset and gorgeous coloring of the rippled waters that overspread the pastures. We think of winter as brown or white, and talk of the cold gray skies, but never my lady's rose-bower more brilliant with bloom than this lake of the day with sunset's rainbow hues. Not one rainbow resting here, but thousands ; not fiery red alone, but every softer shade, and the blossoms of a summer scattered far and near. No thought now of January or the nipping cold of mid-winter nights ; no hint of icy waters black and chill, of arctic desolation, and a longing for the fireside light and warmth. Now was winter in a playful mood and wreathed in rare smiles, as sweet as they are rare. Nor was I alone to enjoy it. A song-sparrow breaks the silence, and his infectious glee moves the crested tit to whistle loudly, as if to call up every bird about him, and a wren on the hill-side shouts back to it, " *Glorious !*"

Such winter days are all too short. I tarried until not a trace of color rested upon the waters ; but scarcely less beautiful were the reflected stars and crescent moon that gilded the black waters of the short-lived lake.

Heard on the Hill-Side.

BUT little that we meet with bears a very close inspection. A gem without a flaw does not flash from every finger; but he is unwise who spends his days hunting for the world's defects. The face of the long, low bluff, that every one calls a hill-side, is not perfect. The moss is in patches, the trees crooked, the bare earth shows in spots, and is gullied and wrinkled where we would have it smooth. The springs flow as they choose and make here a swamp and leave it a desert there. Tell the whole truth, and the face of the long, low bluff is a veritable eyesore. Is it? Even during these early April mornings I find it a very gate of Paradise, if not that fabled garden of delight. Others can find fault if they will, and much joy come to them. But while yet the day was very young the sun peeped over the roof of my neighbor's barn, and in response to the assuring warmth here and there chirped the cheerful chickadee. This is one of the day's minor incidents we should all see and hear. It conveys a useful hint to those pessimistically disposed. It brings out the full meaning of the day. It means wholesome appreciation. He who faces the coming day whistling is not likely to look upon sunset weeping. Later, my little bird uttered the *phœbe* note, as Thoreau calls it, but I hold it says, *Hear me.* Whether or not, I listened. Wind cold as charity roared in the tree-tops; but why mind it? *Hear me !* was the sweet sunrise salutation of the chickadee, and I half believed that some herald of approaching spring had charmed the tangled green brier and added brightness to the mosses. *Hear me !* and, heeding the command, I strolled along the hill-side.

A squirrel barked, but must we take the first greeting as indicative of a disappointing day because it is a surly one? It matters little if a cross-grained squirrel is rude. There is generally some discordant note whatever the conditions or wherever we happen to be. Jays are pretty sure to screech when the matins of the white-throated sparrows are floating along this peaceful hill-side, a hymn to stir the better feel-ings of the most indifferent.   Hearing blue-jays at such a time, it becomes quite evident that a bird's song was not intended for man's enjoy-ment, as has been seriously asserted.   Never-theless, we can get a great deal of satisfaction out of it, sharing the music with the birds with-out robbing them.   But I did not come to the hill-side to philosophize over bird-song, but to listen, and let it be understood that there is an art of listening.   There is no such thing as a meaningless sound.   It is a contradiction to speak of what we hear as having no significance, but the meaning of any sound may or may not be of importance to us.   The footstep of a detective may not disturb our day-dreams, but bring a vision of the gallows to the pursued criminal.   As a matter of fact, the nearest to meaningless sounds are those made by man. Compare for a moment his clumsy tread with the scarcely detected footsteps of a wood-mouse. The man is absolutely nothing to us ; would not be missed, if never heard of ; but the day was never long enough to watch a dainty white-footed wood-mouse pick its way through the dead branches scattered by the storms of the past winter.   If it squeaks when startled, why? Follow the actions now of the mouse and trace the cause of the sound to the shadow of the hawk you see sailing over you.   To simply hear a sound is not all.   To listen, to realize the full intent and purpose of every variation in the sound, to note the accompanying gesture with each characteristic utterance, whenever possible ; in short, to appreciate the effort on an animal's or bird's part to interpret its own feelings, this is to listen intelligently, and in so doing to be taught a useful lesson in ornithology.   There is profit, then, as well as pleasure in being abroad on a bright April morning like this, and noting, whether we stroll along the foot-path way or stand by some one of the old oaks, whatsoever is to be heard on the hill-side.

But the skies are not always bright.   We have heard much of tearful April, and of the showers that are so common during the month ; but the effect of these varying conditions upon bird-life does not appear to have been closely observed. Cloudiness is not necessarily a drawback to a day.   There must be low temperature, chilly dampness, and an east wind to make the early spring migrants mope. I have sometimes thought that the wood-thrush at no later period sang as sweetly as during a dark, cloudy April day, when the leafless woods were filled with that strange shadowless light, such as we see in a Claude Lorraine glass. It is a light to stir the soul of man, if he has any, and could not fail to affect our incomparable poet, the wood-thrush.

What is to be heard on a bright April morning? There is a deal of scepticism on this subject, and the common reply is, I fancy, "Nothing much," or, perhaps, "Crows." Well, I pity the person who can find no pleasure in the varied calls and alarm-notes of these wily birds. It suggests a lack of retrospective power, and much is lost when the restless crows of April do not recall these same birds in the past winter, when all their ingenuity was taxed to gain a living ; and what a pretty sight, when the river opened, to see them riding on huge cakes of ice or deftly darting between them for some coveted morsel with all the grace of the gulls with which they fraternized. But, then, there are people who never see crows except those in their own cornfields. What, then, is to be heard in April? Just a round dozen of good musicians and a host of pleasing *dilettanti* that fill up the unoccupied moments, like gossipy friends between the acts. The dozen are all good, to my mind, but necessarily of varying merit, and more than one, as a soloist, excellent ; while others, in this light, are not, perhaps, to be commended. But let the rambler judge for himself. To-day there were, in varying numbers, robins, Carolina wrens, crested tits, blue-jays, song-sparrows, red-winged blackbirds, cardinal red-birds, vesper sparrows, meadow-larks, chickadee, flicker, and purple grakles, and the united voices of at least three or four, and often twice as many, could be heard at once. An orchestral performance that sometimes was bewildering and occasionally mildly irritating, but never exasperating. It was the birds' way of saluting a morning in April, and they asked neither for permission nor approval. Is it strange that, to-day, the violets opened their eyes and looked towards the skies, and the pale, trembling spring beauty was flushed with excess of joy? Man, in his inordinate conceit, would doubtless have differently arranged matters, and ordered more solos by the cardinal and song-sparrow, or duets by the crested tit and vesper birds, but man should remember that on all such occasions he is an uninvited guest, and ought at least to have sufficiently good manners not to criticise—only he hasn't! Lord of creation, no doubt, but in many a way he makes a pretty mess of it.

April showers! There is nothing depressing about them, and if I ventured to criticise our spring-tide and its birds, it would be that our April shower might be a little repressing so far as the robins are concerned. They certainly are too noisy. A typical shower now fairly electrifies the north-bound warblers, and without exaggeration they can be likened to honey-bees just before they swarm. I have tried more than once to count the warblers in my door-yard elm, but gave up in despair. Possibly the most noticeably excited bird, after an April shower, is the peewee. This is in part because, later in the season, the bird is methodical and emotionless, if not positively melancholy. Not so when the nest is again in order. Their new year has commenced, and after perhaps two or three days of dry and dusty weather, let these be followed by an afternoon shower, and this in turn by a flood of golden sunshine through the dripping trees, and it is a peewee's holiday, or, more strictly speaking, holy hour. Then the two short notes are lengthened into song, and so rapidly repeated that stirring music fills the freshened air, and we know that spring is here. The few new leaves of the hardiest shrubs make green all creation at such a time. If far away from the peewee's home, you have something closely akin to this sudden accession of excitability and emphasized bird-song, after an April shower, in the song and movements of the dainty little field-sparrow. This delightful bird feels strongly the influence of the passing shower, and sings so much more vigorously than usual that I believe its song can be heard at twice as great a distance. Those of us who rush in-doors at the appearance of rain lose a great deal, and more, again, in not taking a hint from the birds and rushing out of doors as soon as the last drop has fallen. Be it birds or business, not one man in a million is too soon on the spot.

The birds of the hill-side this morning recalled a curious specimen of humanity I met with the other day.   I asked him why he never came to these old strolling grounds of his ; that they had not changed for the worse in any way. His reply was, "Oh, there is nothing new to be found there."   His idea of an outing was to collect something new to the neighborhood, plant or animal.   All his out-door world condensed in that one word, "specimen."   To think, as he does, that there are no violets except the one in his herbarium ; no birds, except the distorted skins that disfigure his study. Horrible !   After all, it is the life that attracts us, and not the body that merely displays it, and we have not the whole truth until both body and soul are set before us.   An ornithological museum and a graveyard have a vast deal in common, and I prefer the lively sparrow on the village green to its defunct cousin behind glass doors, as I do my friends of to-day to the crumbling remains of worthy ancestors.

But a truce to controversy, and what more

of the hill-side? An abundance of bird-song largely compensates for lack of leaves, and the trees did not appear bare. The birds sang so much of summer coming that I fancied summer was here; but, in fact, the trees were not bare. The maples are in full bloom; so, too, the elms. Spicewood fairly glitters with its wealth of golden flowers, and tiny tips of green show on many a sheltered shrub. Even the oaks have lost their wintry nakedness. The leaf-buds have swollen, and, as the tree-top shows against the sky, there is a promise of vigorous growth that our imagination helps upon its way. Listening to the birds, we enter into their hopeful, prophetic spirit, and, forgetting the past, we magnify the present, and, looking down the long stretch of forest on the hill-side, gaze, as we fancy, far into the future. What a museum would that be which could give the dweller in town the songs of our birds by merely opening a glass case! The inventor's cunning has come near, but not quite accomplished this. A song may be bottled up, but the sweetness is lacking when you draw the cork, or is it that the songs and the surroundings cannot be dissociated?—a kinship between our lungs and ears, and so a breathing of musical odors as well as hearing of sweet sounds. We cannot be passive, or mere receptacles of impressions that have not for us their real significance. Such cannot be positive even that they heard a bird sing. Think of being only vaguely impressed with the idea that you heard some voices when out of doors! Nevertheless, this is as far as many of my neighbors go.

It profits nothing to draw an invidious distinction, as it really is, when many birds are singing. Too much cannot be said of any bird when that one is in its place, but our extravagance as to the thrushes too often leads to injustice as to some unpretentious sparrow. Not one of the many birds upon the hill-side shall be first to me. I am rich when the least of them sings in my hearing.

As the day draws to a close, all reluctantly I turn my face homeward, and with unwilling steps retrace the day's ramble. The foot-path way is not bathed in the same cheerful light, and the songs that still are heard are less full

of cheer ; or, is the change only in ourselves ?
But merry or melancholy any strain, it is with
a feeling of time well spent that I take back
with me, not specimens, burdens upon both
arm and conscience, but the soul of every
sweet song heard while I lingered on the hill-
side.

Blunders in Bird-Nesting.

THIS is an ill-chosen title, perhaps, yet it is purposely selected because it affords an opportunity to express an opinion on the subject of man's attitude towards bird-life. Bird-nesting in the sense of destroying or disturbing a bird's nest is a crime, and the blunder is on the part of the criminal, who degrades himself. Science, under whose name so much cruelty takes shelter, is no adequate shield to the wretch who deliberately destroys a nest. The maturing of a brood concerns the community, but the color of the eggs and structure of the nest are not matters of transcendent importance, and can be determined without interfering with the rights of the birds.

But the blunders I have in mind, if such they are, are those of the birds themselves; errors of judgment, as seen from our standpoint. As an instance, there are at this time three nests of song-sparrows on the ground in my lane, which runs in a nearly north-and-south direction. These nests are on the west side, and are tilted so as to get the full benefit of the sun in the forenoon. Each nest is deftly concealed by the dead grass of the past summer being drawn over it, and to two of the three are short roofed runways, better built than many I have seen made by a meadow-lark. So far, the birds have been wise, but in all three cases the nests have been placed dangerously near the wagon-track,—in one case within fifteen inches of a deep rut, and the others much less than twice that distance away. The result is, the bird is forced, or so it supposes, to leave the nest every time a carriage passes, and this is quite frequently during the day. Likewise, the sitting bird hurries away on the approach of every foot-passenger. These annoyances and real sources of danger were doubtless not considered when the sites were chosen, and perhaps were unheeded during nest-construction, but the facts must have dawned upon the builders before the eggs were laid. Why, then, they took the apparent risk is incomprehensible to us. From a man's point of view, these birds blundered. In their six little heads was not enough wit to foresee in time inevitable consequences. For many days I have been trying to see what were the compensating advantages of these three similar nest-sites, and I have not been able to solve the problem. However, the three broods were reared successfully, and perhaps this will be held as an evidence that it was I and not the birds that blundered.

But birds not only do blunder occasionally, but acknowledge the fact. I have been daily going the rounds of many nests in all sorts of places, and spent many an hour patiently watching the building of the nest. The Baltimore oriole has more than once commenced a nest on a still day, but found that the wind preceding a summer shower caused too much motion, and the unfinished structure was abandoned. One pair of robins fixed upon a cozy hollow in an apple-tree, but, having no roof overhead, they found their nest in a pool of water after a night's rain. Nevertheless, all else being favorable, birds are willing to risk possible discovery rather than relinquish a position that pleases them. An uncle of mine told me that he took an old crook-neck gourd in which wrens had a nest, gradually moved it nearer and nearer the kitchen door, and finally hung it to one of the bare rafters overhead. The wrens protested, of course, and yet were not willing to be beaten if they could help it. They raised the first brood of that summer in the kitchen, but found a new nesting-place for their second brood. The following summer, so Uncle Timothy said, the wrens came back and inspected the gourd in the kitchen, but concluded to take no risks. As my uncle was a geologist, of course the story may be slightly colored, but I have confirmation of the essential facts.

But, as birds have other enemies than man, it is surprising how much they leave to chance, running risks which, from our point of view, might easily be avoided. For several days I watched a pair of robins that chose as a nesting-site the swaying twigs of a tall pine-tree. Day after day I watched and wondered, and with every puff of wind expected to see the nest come tumbling to the ground. But all went well in those airy regions, and never were two robins happier, if we can judge by their actions. When the nest was finished and probably an egg or two laid, the end came. I happened to be out of doors in the night, and, while looking at the tree-tops darkly limned against the moonlit sky, saw an owl floating in mid-air like a black cloud. Suddenly it swooped down. The robins screamed, and then there was death-like silence. One of the birds was seized, the other was frightened from its home, and the deserted nest remains a monument to their folly. What advantage there could be in a nest in such a position is not demonstrable. True, we do not see the world with a bird's eyes, but we are supposed to have a keener mental if not physical vision, and we must think that the birds blundered. They of course had a purpose in building where they did, but lacked foresight to the extent of not realizing possible disadvantages. Do such birds, escaping death, profit by experience, or repeat their folly? Probably, with them, thought-transference does not go far enough to permit the giving of advice, and improvement can lie only in the one direction of experience. I think there is satisfactory evidence of this, but it is of such a character as not to be convincing when put upon the printed page. A good deal of our ornithological knowledge must be the result of personal observation, and, while this is ever food for thought and a delightful subject of contemplation when we happen to be alone, its bloom is rubbed off, its significance is lessened, its value is depreciated, when subjected to the criticism of others who have not seen as you have seen, or, as so often happens, have not seen at all.

A Morning in May.

I WAS laughed at not long ago for suggesting that the other months resign in favor of May. It is not, after all, so very surprising that such a thought should come, when we consider how full to overflowing is this perfect month. That June day of which Lowell has so sweetly sung did not excel a recent morning, when the humming-birds brought to a close the long procession of north-bound warblers, themselves last and least. The sun rose very slowly over my neighbor's woods, as if it, too, would like to tarry here on the blooming meadows and play bo-peep with the hill-side shadows. The wakeful robin was astir at dawn, and far off in some leafy glade a tuneful thrush piped in its own enchanting way, and soon, roused by these, one by one, the summer's host of songsters joined in the chorus. It is not worth the while to claim which is the earliest bird to sing, nor which first to settle down to the prosy facts of life after the sun has risen. A bird's day and ours are not the same, and he knows the birds best who keeps the same hours. Such things vary indefinitely, too, and a sleepy-head occasionally is the earliest astir, just as no two mornings are alike, even if wind and weather have remained unchanged since yesterday. At least, there will be a variation in the clouds, and the shadow of a cloud may postpone the song of a bird. Clouds and the shadow of a single cloud have been quite too much neglected. I have seen busy nest-building birds suddenly quit work and sit as moodily as if in the depths of despair because the sunlight was shut off, and resume their labors with most suggestive promptness when the sun shone again. It would be difficult to explain this. I have no intention of attempting it; but after seeing it, time and again, for years, there is an almost unavoidable disposition on the rambler's part to spend an hour or two in speculation as to the status of the bird's emotions. Birds' nests we know, and birds we think we know, but not too much attention has been paid to birds when building.   Then, if ever, can we witness the varied manifestations of all their mental qualities.   Love, fear, anger, jealousy, obstinacy, and ingenuity are exhibited in quick succession, and every emotion so unmistakably that there is next to no danger of misinterpretation.   I went the rounds almost daily of forty-two birds' nests during the month, and the many quaint incidents I witnessed would fill a volume: pathetic beyond my power of description where an accident happened to the mate of a redstart; almost complete paralyzation through fear when I attempted to photograph a nest full of young; rage that overreached itself on the part of a Carolina wren I teased; strange antics ascribable only to jealousy when I placed a mirror near a nest, and a catbird saw in its reflected self a rival; persistence when one bird determined to retain material for a nest which the other bird deemed unsuitable; and in how many ways did birds strive to overcome little difficulties I placed in their way! Happily, all went well at last, and these birds and their babies came to know me. So I think, but others doubt it.   At all events, I could do what others could not, and I have my own opinion of the matter. Whether birds of the out-door world come to distinguish individuals or not, they are very much tamer in some localities than others. This no one will deny. My friends were surprised, at the opening of the nesting season, to see a wren's nest on the porch where people were continually passing; and these wrens seemed to know the difference between the family and strangers; but later in the season a pair of wrens took possession of a little watering-pot hung against the side of the house, within arm's length of the pump. A nest was built and a brood reared within six feet of a farm-house kitchen door. I had heard strange stories of very tame house-wrens before, and I am better prepared to believe them now. Do we not too often consider as unusual some incident to which our attention is particularly called? We relate it as an anecdote of animal life, and think it a remarkable illustration of some mental or instinctive quality of the bird or animal, when in fact it is an every-day occurrence. What we see done is not likely to be at all unusual. Under peculiar circumstances any creature may exercise to a greater degree some one of its powers to meet the demands of the occasion, but there is really nothing remarkable in this. It would be strange if they did not, and we would have cause for wonderment if wild life succumbed without an effort to avoid any danger suddenly sprung upon it. When we read anecdotes of animal life, we read usually the every-day doings of the creatures mentioned. When we see these incidents paraded in news-papers as remarkable, we read the evidence of the author's ignorance. It is the manner of the bird or mammal when nothing particular is going on that gives us a true insight as to what that mammal or bird really is, just as we can realize what our friends are only when they are seen unmoved by anger or undisturbed by petty vexations. In birds in particular it is the toss of the head, the flirt of the tail, the cheerful or impatient chirp, and a dozen or more little details that are really instructive and come to the rambler to mean more than all the un-usual incidents, so called, that will be witnessed in a lifetime.

The free agency of birds is as much a myth

as is that of man. Generalizations as to mornings in May, as of many another matter of
Nature, are of no particular value, but of one
recent morning I can speak with confidence, for
haply I was astir at dawn. The robin started
a little trickling stream of song down the hill-
side, and before it had crossed the meadows
and reached the river this same trickling stream
was swollen to a flood of melody. There was
not a silent second for three full hours; not a
moment unburdened with sweet sound. Had
the rambler been in pursuit of some single
song; had he wished to hear the rose-breasted
grosbeak, or one of the vireos, or desired to
single out the utterance of some migratory warbler, his efforts would have proved in vain. This
bewildering confusion of infinitely varied sounds
cannot in its entirety be considered, in a scientific sense, as music. An orchestra would be
mobbed that attempted to reproduce it; so,
why is it that the birds' salutation to the rising
sun does not offend the ear? It is true, I have
heard of a musician who swore at a nightingale
and exclaimed "What discord!" but the world
at large has thousands of less critical ears, and

such are pleased, not pestered, when a wild bird sings. Everything, I take it, depends upon the surroundings. In an aviary, for instance, the same mingled bird-songs would not be attractive. The medley in a bird-store, canaries and parrots, is never musical, but who unaffectedly objects to the mingled voices of a dozen birds in their own home? Even the crow's cawing blends with the thrush's song, and we have not mere discord,— the rambler has not, at least,—but mingled wildness and melody; the rugged and the tender; activity and contemplation. The truth is, if we find such harsh sounds as that of the crow and qua-bird and the fretful *whough* of the green heron a source of annoyance, then we lack that trace of the savage in our nature that is like the pinch of salt that makes the dish of meat palatable. There is something that amuses me and really calls for pity when I see a man or woman ecstatic over the warbling of a rose-breast and given to scolding if a blue-jay screams. I have known my visitors to shrug their shoulders when, in the course of a ramble, we stopped at the flood-gates, and instead of songs of thrushes, heard the rattle of the king-

The old flood-gates.

fishers.   For longer than I can remember these birds have made the creek at the ruins of the flood-gates their favorite summer home, and the "rattle" that disturbs the visitor is music to me, because of old associations.   Remember, you have gone to Nature, not coaxed her to come to you, and where she is there expect to find her just as she is.   There will be no hurried opening of a stuffy parlor as you approach ; no thrusting of this into the background and pushing that to the fore, nor frantic effort to change a dress in time.   There will be no flushed face, due to haste, ill concealed by powder, but an honest countenance, and no shadow of annoyance at your appearance.   Nature is ever ready to meet the right kind of visitors ; is not taciturn or petulant ; but by not so much as a hair's-breadth will she vary from a predetermined course.   The birds are hers, not ours, and if she bids them all sing at the same moment, remember, she is directing her own orchestra for her own entertainment and never even so much as remembers there is such a thing as a man on earth.   Like a conscientious student, she has due regard for the law of priority, and being herself older than the birds, and birds ages older than the dawn of humanity, she rightly considers that man, Nature's most recent afterthought, should be a respectful listener only and not assume to dictate. Even to offer advice is impudent, and to presume to criticise ill-mannered. The rejoicing of the birds of a morning in May is no novelty to the time-worn hill-side along which I wander. The sweetness thereof has drifted like a cloud in the summer sky from the forest to the river, from the river to the sea,—a sweetness that has soothed many a troubled breast in the days of our forefathers and calmed my own fretfulness to-day.

But a morning in May is not merely a matter of bird-song. There enters into it bird activity as well, and to the practised eye this activity, in its various phases, is as characteristic of birds as is their singing. Birds of different species are alike in some ways, but are also, on the other hand, as unlike as we are. What among mankind is called a family trait or peculiarity has its analogue in the differences among species. It is possible to recognize a bird by the wing movement or flirt of the tail, its method of flight, or general manner when at rest or walking, but when it becomes a matter of positive identification such minor details are not to be trusted ; the risk is too great. Imitations too often occur, as in bird-song. Birds that are not tree creepers can creep over trees, and birds without webbed feet can swim like a duck when necessity requires it.

It is apparent, from all this, that to be abroad at sunrise is no blind man's holiday, the world open only to our ears. There is ever much to see as well as to hear ; but we stand, as it were, on dangerous ground if moved to report all we witness. Some one, neither able to see nor hear, might, from the controversies arising, doubt if either faculty was developed among his fellows.

The enjoyment of watching birds comes from our attempts to interpret their actions. We can go but a little way. We know if a bird is eating or drinking, but when it is at rest the question arises, Is it thinking ? It may be said that the bird is strictly passive, and so only roused to action by some external stimulant. It sees an insect and pursues it ; but if no insects come in sight for a protracted time, then, to avoid starvation, an instinct to travel is roused by the cravings of an empty stomach. I cannot incline to a view that makes of the bird merely a machine. There is one feature of the year limited hereabouts to the closing days of April and the beginning of May,—the return of migratory birds. It is unquestionable that, to a certain extent, we have the same individuals return year after year. There is no confusion when they arrive; no restless wandering to and fro; no crowding, as when emigrants are herded on the steamer's wharf. The wrens go to their boxes, the rosebreasts to the orchard, the oriole to the elm, the indigo-bird to the shrubbery, the swifts to the chimney, the peewee to its nesting-site under the bridge. There is no confusion, but orderly return to the routine of a year ago. This immediate distribution, each bird to its particular haunt of the preceding year, could scarcely come about if there was, on the part of the birds, a total ignorance of the locality; nor is there any delay in finding materials for nest-building, but this, of course, is not so strange, but there is some significance in the fact that when material was provided in a previous year, this is remembered and the same spots promptly visited. I have aided many an oriole and great crested flycatcher when building commenced, and the aid extended and accepted then seemed the following spring to be expected, which I submit as proof positive that I was dealing with the same birds. A little chippy, the hair-bird, has accepted my offering of waxed coarse sewing-silk as a nest lining and does not trouble itself to hunt for hairs. I hope, if my pets of the box-bush live long enough, that they will take the silk directly from my hands. The wrens of my porch have more than once raided my wife's work-basket, and it was indeed a funny sight when one of them stepped upon a cushion and was pricked by a needle. Half, I think, of the delight of watching the birds that return to us in May is to realize that they are in great measure our friends of other years. This fact makes it practicable to go directly to the chosen homes of any species. We lose no time, and happiness would be complete were fear banished from the bird's breast and the word "wild" marked obsolete in the dictionary. It is steadily decreasing among the birds of the door-yard, but we cannot rest content not to wander beyond its confines ; and no time like a May morning to plunge into the farthest thicket, tread the most dismal swamp,

and trace old pathways through the darkest woods, eager as ever to see and hear, and, hearing and seeing, to solve the various problems of bird nature ; problems ever set before us, when out of doors, but never in such bewildering profusion as when we start early on our rambles when the woods are greening and violets fleck the dewy pastures.

Dinner at Noon.

THERE is a great deal in the way we divide our day, and, absurd as such a thing may seem at first thought, there is something to be said in defence of dinner at noon. Of course everything depends upon what portion of each twenty-four hours is set aside for sleep ; but it can scarcely be called irrational to select the half-dozen least suggestive hours, and these are the year round from 10 P.M. to 4 A.M. Not that we miss nothing by being then asleep, for every hour has its own wonderful history, but, the year through, we lose least by turning our backs upon the world at such a time.

Dinner at noon means an early breakfast,— preposterously early to many people ; but why not follow Nature a little more closely than we do and get our share of the fruits of the morning? A strawberry, while yet the dew is upon it, is one of the marvels of Nature's handiwork, and our conception of the world about us is broadened almost indefinitely by a closer acquaintance than people usually possess. Strange as it seems, most people that I have met appear to have a horror of sunrise, and boast, not of witnessing this phenomenon, but of having persistently turned their backs upon it. They are welcome to do so. The sun does not feel the slight, and will go on rising quite indifferent to humanity's whims and oddities. It is gravely asserted, too, that there is danger in the unsunned air of early morning, and insanity is the result of too frequent lungfuls of the day at dawn; that farmers lose their sanity because of early rising, and, if not quite so bad as this, at least their mental strength is prematurely weakened. Perhaps the air is poison-laden at dawn, but the toilers in the field are more probably driven insane by over-worry than by overmuch breathing of the morning freshness. Obnoxious politics, rather than obnoxious gases, cause the mischief. Tariff tinkering and stock gambling can and do work greater mischief with the farmer than miasmatic taints that pass his nostrils. It is the all work and no pay, due to pernicious legislation, and not the chill or damp that greets us when we plunge into the odor-laden air of a bright June morning and greet the coming day. The familiar distich concerning "early to bed and early to rise" has as much sense as sound, and this cannot be said of all the rhymes of all our rhymesters. For one, I am willing to run the risks of insanity for the sake of what I hear at sunrise, and in spite of the sneers of aristocracy will eat my dinner at noon; and I hold that man a downright fool who will not judge for himself what is best for his individual needs, or lives under protest that his neighbor may have no occasion to criticise. Our duty to our neighbor does not extend that far. If it did, it were time to revolutionize the world.

If the early morning is so worthy of an intimate acquaintance, why has not the world long ago made the discovery? What I call "the world" has done so, but my world is not yours. Day and night have not the same meaning in the city as they have in the country. I have often wondered if the robin slept with one eye open, for, however indistinct may be the first faint streak of light in the east, it will be detected by this bird, and the approach of day announced in no uncertain tones. The wrens that are nesting near my window are first to hear the news, and, with no further toilet than a wing-shake and a comfortable yawn, repeat it from corner to corner of the house, until I am in no doubt as to the approximate time of day. Then, one by one, the goodly list of birds about us take up the cry, and not a nook or corner of the farm but rings with the tidings that the day is breaking. Why should I not be astir? If the world now is fit for every bird that flies, I will trust to not being out of place. Whether poison or not, I daily risk the morning air for the sake of the morning's music. Breakfast over, I am ready, while yet there is but a broad band of gilded cloud in the east, to take my stand under the old oaks and listen. The leaves still dripping with dew, the meadows hidden by low-lying mist, the noonday world as a sealed book, but music steals from it, and it is for this I came. All the world knows our wood-thrush, and has gone ecstatic over it, so let us pass it by with brief mention. Its melody fills the air now, unceasing as the murmur of the south wind in the tall pines. The songs of many thrushes are now completely filling every moment, every spot to which we wander. We breathe the music as we do the odor of the many blossoms. An all-pervading song of such subtle sweetness is it that pleasure gives way at last to a feeling akin to pain,—sweetness that is sad rather than cheerful; the continued telling of a sorrowful story, of love lost rather than of love triumphant.

How very different the song of the rose-breasted grosbeak! Not even those very learned people, the professional ornithologists, appear to have heard it. At least, judging from the literature of the subject, these birds have been heard only to hum, to talk with their fellow-grosbeaks, and whistle a few notes as if to refresh their recollection of some special effort; but the song proper, the melodic outburst of flute-like notes, notes that, by their magic, silence other birds and will stay the steps of any mortal not a fool, —these appear not to be generally known: grand, exultant, the peroration of cheerfulness, the perfect hymn of absolute content. Hearing this, the impression of a thrush's supremacy is changed. But such is not the only song of this superb singer. When in a meditative mood this grosbeak has a song that we fancy is retrospective, so far as the singer is concerned. It is pitched in so low a key that we must be near to hear it, and while we listen and watch the bird the thought comes to us that now the grosbeak is studying some new effort, one of transcendent merit, and it is no wonder that we do, for this low, meditative strain is one of incomparable sweetness, as if the soul of a flute murmured in its dreams.

In all such outings we are too apt to ignore the minor minstrelsy that goes so far to perfect a summer morning. By actual count, I recently heard singing at the same time, or so nearly so as to give that impression, fifteen species of birds, and there are several others that I have found nesting within a comparatively short distance. Not all of these are accounted song-birds, that is, musical in a marked degree, but their efforts, heard with others, go to make up a chorus that is inspiriting, that makes you believe in cheerfulness as a gift of great value.

The great crested flycatcher can do nothing but cacophonously screech, and it teases more than any ear-piercing fife, but when the sound is mingled with the rustling of leaves, the united voices of summer warbler, redstart, and yellow-throat, or of Carolina wren or cardinal red-bird, it adds a decided flavor of wildness to the whole, and so is quite acceptable. All music is to me mere sound, if not suggestive, and many a noise that is crude and disagreeable in one locality may be pleasing in another. The roar of Niagara is readily imitated, but without Niagara is nothing but noise. The common crow's considerable vocabulary is but a series of harsh cries if the poor bird is caged at the Zoo ; but given a crisp October morning, with the forest draped in scarlet and the far-off skies of incomparable blue,—hear this same crow now, when perched on some tall tree-top, its rhythmic call keeping time to the dropping of nuts and rustling of falling leaves,—hear then this much-maligned bird, and you are listening to music that will linger long in your memory.

To become the better acquainted with our birds, for no second-hand knowledge is so unsatisfactory, and at times exasperating, as the recorded impressions of some other observer, whether amateur or professional, it is necessary not only to see and hear birds collectively, but to single out some one of them as it flashes by you, and follow it as best you can. You must go on the "faint heart never won fair lady" principle; go determined to follow through thick and thin. This seems much easier to say than do, but the rambler will find his way very seldom insuperably blocked. Time and civilization have about obliterated the pathless forest or impenetrable thicket, at least on this side of the Mississippi River. Our wildest wilderness is generally a rather tame affair, so it is not a desperate undertaking to go to the edge of a swamp, and, by going, you will see what a picture some small bird in which you are interested makes of a mere mud-hole, some otherwise desolate spot, shaded by rank weeds, and giving off malarial odors. Here, to your infinite surprise, you will be greeted by songs that you have not previously heard, or heard indistinctly, as when a yellow-throat transforms acknowledged ugliness to accepted beauty by virtue of the creature's earnest but not unmusical warbling of such words as *witchery, witchery, witch!* Plunge into some thicket and shut yourself from the world by a surrounding wilderness of twiggy growths, and meet face to face a Carolina wren. The bird may be a bit surprised at

your intrusion, but it really does not mean disrespect if, as is likely, it demands, "How'd ye get here?" with startling emphasis, and follows the question with a peremptory "Get out, get out, get out!" You will be astonished at first, then amused, and so entertained that the apparent rudeness will have no depressing effect, and on reaching the open country and again in a beaten path, you will wonder why you have never been so inquisitive as to birds before.

In a morning's outing worthy of the name, if in early summer, the chances are that you will find a bird's nest as you trace the narrow paths of the wood or break one for yourself through a thicket,—perhaps the nest of a small flycatcher or of one of the vireos, adepts in the art of catching flies. Pretty structures these that bear close examination, for they are skilfully built, and no little engineering skill has been brought to bear upon their construction that the wind and rain may not destructively prevail against them. Perhaps a shrill buzzing, as of an angry bee, may startle you, and again and again you look, but in vain, for your assailant. It is an irate humming-bird, whose nest you have unwittingly approached. If you look long and patiently you may find the latter, saddled on some horizontal branch, looking like a small lichen-coated excrescence, but fashioned with infinite care. Such nest-hunting does the birds no harm, and you return from your tramp amply rewarded, and, it may be safely added, mentally refreshed. Not a bird that does not repay the rambler for all his trouble in following it into its most secret haunts. You are always instructed as well as entertained, and more sure of seeing and hearing wisdom of act and utterance than when with crowds of men ; for while there is no bird that does not make mistakes, they are never such lifelong blunderers as ourselves. After an early morning outing, you return with a deeper insight into the world about you and discover fountains of pleasure-giving knowledge that had hitherto been unsuspected, though perhaps during all your life within easy reach.

But what has all this to do with dinner at noon? Do you remember that my outings commence at dawn, and I feel tardy if not in advance of the rising sun? It is not strange that, old as I am, I still cling to that delight of childhood, a bite between meals, fit subject, by the way, for a reminiscential essay, and, as midday draws near, am ready for a substantial meal. Dinner at noon is not, from this point of view, to be sneered at. And after it? As nature takes a nooning, birds are silent, flowers sleep, and even the brook seems to dally drowsily with the pebbles that fret its course, why not follow their example? A noonday meal, a mid-day nap, and then ready to meet the world on even terms. I am receptive to the renewed activities of the closing day. In short, dinner at noon means two short days rather than one long period of activity in the twenty-four hours ; and who, when a child, but did not always prefer two pieces of pie rather than one big one? It seemed more, whether it was or not, and that made all the difference in the world. Let what is before us seem superlatively excellent and so it is, in that mightiest sense, unto our own selves.

The Poetry of Shelter.

IT requires no labored mental effort to comprehend the philosophy of shelter; but what of this necessity of our lives in its poetical aspect? That it has such an aspect may, indeed, be asked, and it is not strange that there should be serious doubts as to its existence. But shelter is a good deal more than the roof and walls of your accustomed home; much more than the protection of some awning, or umbrella, or the open doorway of a friend's house, however welcome you may be therein. Daily and in innumerable ways we are taking shelter, even to the seeking it, from the results of our blunders, in ways that are open to question.

But all this is prosy to the point of dulness. Happily, on the other hand, for some at least, it is a positive pleasure to turn from the civilized to the savage, from the formal and fixed to the unrestrained and circumstanced by chance only,

as when, overtaken by a storm, we seek some
shelter in the country, in perhaps a true wilderness,—an effective shelter wherein we are safe
from the discomfort or possible danger incident
to exposure, and, while unconcerned as to ourselves, can contemplate Nature in her fretful or
positively angry mood, whether a gentle rain or
a driving storm prevails; for there is almost as
much difference between a summer shower and
a cloud-burst as between bathing and drowning.
We are much too far from Nature when at home
during a rain. The world as seen from the
windows even of a country house is too much
like the moon seen through a telescope. Realizing that there are mountain-tops, we long to
stand upon them. Distance does not always
lend enchantment to the view. A far-off tree,
to come to tamer things, is a disturbing sight
until I have wandered through the wilderness
of its tangled branches. A hollow in any tree
frets me until I have seen the owl that lives
therein. I would knock at the doors of all my
neighbors that are not burdened with humanity,
and see if life has not features among them that
might by adoption lessen the load that I am

Where old Poaetquissings widens to a little lake.

doomed to carry. On the other hand, to attempt to withstand the fury of a raging tempest as does the lonely chestnut in a pasture or the old oak by the roadside is foolhardy. We need adequate shelter, but its value is in proportion to its simplicity. A hollow sycamore has been my safe harbor more than once, and, standing therein while it rained, I felt as an owl must feel, and went home hooting my satisfaction, not humanly shouting it.

As an episode in a rainy-day ramble, give me an overturned boat under which I can lie while the shower passes. There is rare pleasure in living for a few moments like a meadow-mouse. To be one with the wildness about us is an unending joy, for the memory is too much impressed to have the pictures fade, though you live as long as the myths of tradition. Well I remember, how long ago it boots not to tell, being overtaken by a sudden shower while drifting with the current where old Poaetquissings widens to a little lake. Quickly the little craft was turned inshore, and just as the initial pounding drops came rattling down the boat was tilted nearly over and I was safely ensconced beneath it. Never was the creek more beautiful to my faithful eyes, for to my mind Nature has nowhere else been so lavish of her charms. The rain fell in huge drops, that struck the water like pebbles, making a glittering splash, for the storm was local in its strictest sense and the sun shone brightly in the western sky. While lying in my snug retreat I saw a pretty wood-duck with her brood moving by in fancied security, as if no harm would come while it was raining. Presently the duck stopped, turned, and faced me, as if it purposed sharing my shelter. How my heart beat ! I feared the duck would hear my breathing. Suddenly when very near it stopped, and I could plainly see its bright black eyes. The young gathered about, and the group rested as content as I was under the boat. The shower was now over and I was anxious to continue on my journey, but could not miss such an opportunity to see these wary birds. After some chattering, a rather melodious "peeping" by the young, the parent duck led them back to the middle of the creek. I crawled from my hiding-place, and the moment I stood up the mother disappeared and the young flapped the water for several seconds until white with foam ; then all were gone. Splatter-dock and arrow-head were here above the water, which was so shallow I think the birds escaped by hiding rather than diving. Many a time since then I have sheltered myself in this or some similar way and watched the creek for hours.   It is hard upon one's muscles, but I never remember my patience to have gone unrepaid.   To keep yourself hidden is the secret of success in observing wild life.   By so doing you gather in an hour more practical natural history than by any other plan that I have tried or know of others trying.   It is astonishing how often aquatic life comes to the surface ; and it is something to see even the heads of turtles, snakes, eels, frogs, and perhaps a mink comes inshore with a fish in his jaws. Taking shelter in some chance way from a passing tumult in the overarching skies, we happily forget, for the time, the crushing weight of our own importance as man, and see with the clearer vision and interpret with the unprejudiced wit of the purely animal.   Nothing so surely rids us of our sense of importance as to find the storm no respecter of persons, and to be forced, like any bird of the air or beast of the field, to seek the nearest shelter.   With no time allowed us for selection, we accept the first offer of a shield from the pitiless storm, and our thankfulness converts, or should convert, the hovel into a palace.

Herein lies the poetry of shelter.   Contradictory as it may seem, I have been much of late in palatial hovels.   Of course we are never satisfied ; that is out of the question.   Comfortably sheltered from the rain, within arm's length of the best bit of wildness in a day's journey, with birds so near we can see their eyes, and snakes in such proximity we can count their scales, we delude ourselves into thinking such opportunities can be had on demand, and, peering out from our shed, cave, or hollow tree, continually ask ourselves the question, Is it going to clear?   Do our clear-weather days yield us such profit that an occasional rainy one can justly cause us regret?   The anxiety for the storm's cessation had better be set aside for an hour, and the best made of a passing opportunity.   How many pages have been printed of wild life in the rain? Clear-weather men have grown eloquent over clear-weather birds, but what of the thrush that has sought shelter and the hawk that is soaring above the passing clouds? What of the fragile insects that were dancing in the sunbeams and will reappear with the returning sunshine? No naturalist has done full justice to the most commonplace locality. If he would occasionally go abroad with only a pencil and paper and take notes instead of specimens, what a brightening would there be of zoological text-books! The younger men are too eager to increase their collections; the older men find the work too laborious; but a change may come, and he who has best made known the habits of every creature we meet will loom up as greatest among naturalists. There is something very delightful in seeing a woodpecker put his head out of doors, or a thrush peep from a leafy shelter, to see if the rain is over. It is ludicrous to see a frog poke his nose above the surface of the water, ready to croak again, when bang! goes a drop of rain on his head, and down he goes into the depths to wait for perhaps another hour. All animal life appears to know better when it is going to rain than when it is going to clear. It is said that the robin is an excellent weather prophet to this extent, but at times he is wofully mistaken. A lull in the storm is supposed to be the end of it, and the woods ring with the bird's premature rejoicing; and, strange to relate, some people are fooled all their lives by the bird's mistakes, and yet swear to the last that the robin is as safe a guide as the best barometer that man can build. I believe in the robin, but always fortify my belief by carrying an umbrella.

Here is my last experience in a chance shelter, wherein I tarried for two hours, snug as any snail in its shell. I was not tired; I had not walked a dozen miles that day; and yet the idea of stopping for a while was not an annoyance. My aimless wandering had been through neglected pastures, where the cattle were forced to search for the scanty patches of sweet grass, and in so much of the region as had reverted to Nature's care there was all the charm again of Nature's taste. What though the clouds were gathering? The ground-floor of earth was too attractive for me to explore the attic. Clouds might gather and the storm break at last, but I would not for such reason part company with the sparrows in the hedge. And the storm did break. A few admonishing drops came gently down, and, tapping the tough leaves of the oak, made known their mission. It was their business to announce that it was going to rain. Receiving the message, I took shelter in an ideal spot,—in a great hollow willow-tree standing where the creek bends almost at a right angle. This old tree, for years past, has been put to many uses. It has often been the storehouse of picnic parties, and years ago had been used as a stove, the effect of which was to char the walls and roof and make them no longer available as homes of ants, spiders, and uncanny creeping things. I had been here before, and it is ever a pleasure to feel that one is not a stranger. To feel that we are strangers deadens our appreciation of whatever we see. I filled the hollow in the tree without discomfort, and before me was the winding creek, with alternate pasture and woodland reaching to its shore. At the time there was no apparent current, but in a few moments the tide turned.

The twigs and leaves that had passed by returned. Very slowly but steadily the waters crept again over the wide reach of barren mud and up the slimy sides of the stumps of trees felled, it may be, centuries ago,—stumps that might tell strange stories had they tongues. What a delight to talk to a tree that never saw a white man! The rain continued; the sound of the million drops about me was a steady hum that did not deaden other sounds. Far and near were merry-hearted birds that sang sweetly as, like me, they waited for sunshine; but not even the steady dripping of raindrops is monotonous. A gentle breeze stirs to greater activity, and at times there was a roar like that of the surf of the far-off sea.

While waiting and watching, I asked myself, how old is this creek? When did the tide for the first time explore this winding valley? when did the waters of many sparkling springs first greet the sunshine, and, collecting, wander towards the river? Even if we cannot contemplate the end of all things, we are always curious about their beginnings. "At the close of the Glacial period," glibly replies the geologist;

but, cunning as he is, he never ventures upon a more definite statement. Perhaps ten thousand years ago, perhaps ten times ten thousand. The only satisfaction is that we have abundant room for private speculation. It is a genuine pleasure to have a few millenniums to squander and yet keep within bounds. Lord Kelvin tells us the age of the earth may be so much or so much ; only a trifle of thirteen millions of years between the extremes ! Such estimates are not satisfactory. If Crosswicks Creek before me is only ten thousand years old, it is a mere child yet, to be sure, but we can learn a good deal from children. This fluviatile youngster has had several millions of high and low tides, and still can smile serenely whether the day is clear or cloudy. Its ups and downs do not disturb its temper, and this is a fact worth knowing. Do men laugh when it is low tide with them ? Are they never fools at high tide ?

As I watched and waited, I thought of a dead creek I had lately visited,—a creek that had flowed where now is a high, dry, upland field. Running waters are tireless scribes, recording their autobiography up to their last moments. "He who runs must write," is the law of their existence; but "he who comes among men must read," does not hold good. If the record contradicts a careless preconception, then the man is often brazen enough to call Nature an ugly name. An old man who looked on while others were digging went away after hearing much discussion, muttering,—

> "Place little reliance
> On men of science."

I do not wonder. But this creek of other days had its pretty story. It flowed and fretted before Crosswicks Creek came into being. It carried the sand from the adjoining hills and spread it over a plain ; it bore ice with pebbles encased, and dropped the pebbles with as little regularity as plums in a pudding,—often no plums at all, like my piece of pudding when a little boy. Storms occurred in those long-gone days, and the waters were soiled. Mud and clay replaced the clean sand and covered the bed of the one-time stream. Such in brief was the story told ; but there is another chapter. In the sand, and often under layers of clay, were flakes of stone such as man only can produce, and finished blades of stone wherewith man cut his food and fashioned his clothing. We think of our own people as men of a distant past, who came here some two centuries ago,—think of them as seeing this country when it was young and fresh ; and we are quite lost in contemplating the Indian who preceded our ancestors. His is antiquity too great for our decipherment. But now a more remote phase of human activities is laid bare. It is sufficiently plain to those willing to see, and a source of endless amusement when in connection therewith we witness the antics of the overwise who have been proclaiming that such things could not be,—who overvalue theory and undervalue veracity.

The rain is over. The steady hum of the millions of drops has toned down to the dripping of a few thousands. Every leaf holds a few sparkling gems wherewith it is loath to part, but the greedy earth demands every one, and mischievous breezes scatter them over the grass and into the bosom of the swelling tide. Though birds carry no barometers about them, they know when the change has come, and how

promptly do they venture from their shelters !
Not a robin but is shouting now, and the gentler
strains, the refined expressions of sweet content,
such as the song-thrush knows, ring through
the leafy arches of old woods.   Not a redstart
but is on the alert for venturesome flies, not a
greenlet but begins his song in praise of tireless
energy.   It is a strange medley that is now
heard, a confusion that frets us if we have a
preference ; and such is always mine, when
above all these varied songs I hear the rosebreast, whose magic song snaps sorrow's chain.
How few people appear to have heard this bird,
if we may judge from what has been written !
As well say that you have heard some great
master when he was only tuning his violin, as
to claim familiarity with the rosebreast's song
on hearing a few high notes.   A finished performance is the bird's hymn to contemplation,
which the rosebreast withholds from all who
are not very near to it.   The rambler must
share the shelter of the same tree, and then, it
may be, this marvellous musician will take him
into his confidence and warble strains no thrush
need ever hope to echo.

The glittering sunshine calls me out of doors, or, now, from a doorless house, and I do not leave, I trust, unmindful of the merits of this modest shelter. Trees have a new meaning now to me. Not only their leafy branches, but their bodies, offer shelter, so I have more homes on earth than I ever dreamed of. When the storm breaks, a man need not be unhappy in a hollow tree. It affords the protection that he asked, and what more had he a right to expect? But there is also added the goodly gift of delightful suggestiveness.

My Elm-Tree Oriole.

THE humming-bird is summer written in italics ; the scarlet tanager is the season's exclamation point. By nothing else is our delight at summer's charm so well expressed. We never look beyond these birds for greater glory. They are the completion, we feel, of the summer's effort to beautify our woods and by-ways. The Baltimore oriole is a strong competitor. There is the tropical brilliancy and almost the humming-bird's activity, but many soon weary of this display of orange and black, of flame and smoke, because of the tiresome screeching with which its presence is proclaimed. I have known nervous people driven in-doors by the oriole's harsh cries, that can best be likened to the piercing creak of unoiled machinery. But it is not always so. Early in the blessed month of May a smooth-tongued oriole came to the door-yard elm, and with all the vivacity of its

122

race, while threading the maze of branches of this fine old tree, sang in dulcet tones these cheerful words : " Music, good music, all day !" My oriole I called it from the day it came, and when you take to a bird it often happens that the bird will take to you. Not actually, as you might say this of a person, but so it seems in your fancy, and that is practically the same thing. Whether the bird knew me or not, I knew the bird. The elm-tree was not the oriole's only home. It wandered along the hill-side, even to my neighbor's door-yard, and often was so far away that I could scarcely hear the sweet song that so effectually drove away dull care. But these wanderings were always of short duration. The distance was never great as measured by the bird's power of flight, and after a period of comparative silence the bird would suddenly reappear and rouse the very echoes with its inspiring song, " Music, good music, all day !" I say "comparative silence," for silence absolute does not occur. We have but to consider the needs of the birds and they will make return of the best they have to offer, their songs. There are wrens in my boxes and in a corner of my porch. There are cardinal redbirds in my garden, and rose-breasted grosbeaks in the orchard. Song-sparrows nest in the gooseberry-bushes, and robins, thrushes, chats, vireos, and flycatchers tarry wherever they can find a nesting-place, and all are in full song. So it is, therefore, that my elm-tree oriole speaks not for itself only but for them when its clear, flute-like whistle proclaims from dewy morn until the gloaming, " Music, sweet music, all day !"

When in the misty, murky east
  Forbidding clouds are piled,
Fit realms where imps of darkness feast
  And gladness never smiled,
Ere long there comes, despite the glance
  Of night's forbidding frown,
The cheery morning's swift advance,
  And casts her foeman down ;
Then one fair bird, unmoved by fear,
  Speaks to my doubting soul,
Revives my hopes with words of cheer,
  My elm-tree oriole.

The hours pass, the sun in might
  Bids gloomy shadows flee,
As some strange troubling dream, the night
  Has fled beyond the sea.

No merry warbler of the wood,
  No songster of the field,
Hath his heart-stirring warmth withstood,
  To his command they yield.
And songs of love, life's sweetest song,
  Through field and forest roll,
And foremost in the tuneful throng
  My elm-tree oriole.

The shadows of the coming night
  May fill the leafy glen,
The sunny landscape shut from sight
  And darkness reign again,
But not a song of sunny day
  Is lost; we hear them still,
They linger by the foot-path way,
  The meadows, and the hill:
Songs from the hearts of birds as true
  As needle to the pole,
But nearest of them all are you,
  My elm-tree oriole.

Now, having heard this song from time to time during the summer; having seen the bird weave the fabric of a wonderful nest, suspended from the most yielding of the tree's terminal twigs; having seen the young carefully inducted into the wide world with all its delights and dangers, and heard the last regretful chirp of young and old as they leave the home tree for fresh woods and pastures new; even after all this, can we say that we have a thorough knowledge of these birds? I think not. We have as deep waters to fathom as when we deal with mankind, and not only as deep, but different. Bird-nature is not our nature, and it is an open question whether or not it is in our power to rightly interpret the motives of the birds about us. To slaughter them that we may count the fibres of a particular muscle or determine the precise tint of a feather gives us no clue to what most concerns us,—what birds do and why they do it. Perhaps we shall never know; but our present ignorance, of which we are aware, is not painful or at all irritating, when we are striving to overcome it, but really a source of pleasure. We are drawn the more to the birds because of it, ever hopeful of a solution of the problem at last, and if doomed to die, as is probable, without that full light to which we aspire, we have at least had the pleasure of listening, while we labored, to "Music, good music, all day!"

Though almost hourly in evidence, the elm-tree oriole did not overshadow the other birds.

Not a condor of the Andes could thrust my door-step wrens into the shade, nor majestic eagle lessen the glory of that darling of the door-yard, the song-sparrow. I will not attempt to explain it, but the fact stands unmoved and immovable, birds, unlike all other forms of animal life, do not weary us. We may wish, at times, that they were not so noisy, yet his is a brutal hand that would brush them aside. For their many merits we readly overlook such a trivial blemish as excessive loquacity. Think of driving into the deserts all of our own species that talk too much. Who of us would be left?

The literature of the subject, ornithology, covering thousands of pages and hundreds of titles, has heretofore dealt with bird anatomy, classification, and their habits, and only at rarest intervals has a single word gone up in their defence. Because some birds are fruit-eaters, they are proclaimed destructive to our horticultural interests; because crows like very young chickens, the poultry-men are up in arms; and so runs on this sickening twaddle through many chapters. There has been too little said of the other side, as is usual. What of the insects and worms that were sapping the strength of the fruit-trees ; what of the millions of grubs and of destructive cut-worms devoured by the crow ? I have seen the stomach of a crow that proved to be full almost to overflowing with cut-worms that were gathered the very morning of the bird's death at the hands of an obstinate, ignorant, prejudiced farmer in that man's own field. I do not speak strongly without reason.   I have in mind a cherry-tree, bearing phenomenally fine fruit in great abundance.   As soon as there was a trace of blush upon the cherries the robins came and feasted, and, as was claimed, to the entire destruction of the crop.   Not one bird, but several, came, and then the cat-birds followed.   " No pies or puddings ; none to can for next winter,"—these dolorous cries went up throughout the house, and had there been no staying hand, the arms of an arsenal would have been brought to bear upon the offending birds. There was as much mourning in-doors as out in the yard there was " Music, good music, all day !" The day of ripened fruit came at last, and all the one-time mourners feasted ; our neighbors feasted.   We gathered until weary of gathering ;

until every closet was burdened with cherries, canned, pickled, and preserved, and then the unused fruit finally fell from the tree in such quantities that the grass about the tree-trunk was destroyed. The truth was, we had fed the birds and the birds had fed us, and more, they had entertained us. They had sung whenever we appeared, and through that summer there was not a moment when, wearied of the nagging of an exacting world, we could not turn to the birds of the door-yard and be soothed by " Music, good music, all day !"

All birds are a delight to both the eye and ear. I know of no one that is ugly when in its proper place. I know of no one that is discordant when waking the echoes of its own home. The dull brown diver of the mill-pond is a sorry spectacle when waddling over the ground in search of water, but the moment that element is reached all this bird's awkwardness disappears. The herons and bitterns, as they rise from the marsh in anxious haste, seem only desirous of escape, and are merely a jumble of illy-directed wings and legs ; but settled to rhythmic flight, their movements in the upper

air are extremely graceful.   Nearest to being a
blot upon the scene is a too near view of a
turkey-buzzard, particularly if it has just gorged
itself with unsavory food.   Startle such a bird,
and its awkward effort to regain command of
its wings is not only suggestive of Nature having
blundered in this instance, but we are likely to
be amused as well as moved to pity.   But when
this vulture's wings have conquered gravity and
the one-time almost helpless creature passes into
the upper air, our pity becomes envy ; we do
not criticise now, but wonder, and how helpless
we feel ourselves to be, at least in so far as re-
gards locomotion, when we watch that soaring
vulture floating, without an effort, among the
clouds.

The hooting of an owl when we are passing,
it may be in the night, along some lonely woodland path ; the weird cry of the heron, its ghost-
like, guttural " whough !" suddenly breaking
upon our ears ; the far-away iteration of the
whippoorwill, hidden in some leafy dell ; the
shrill, despairing cry of some sleeping bird
roused to sudden realization of danger and of
death,—such sounds as these may not be ac-

counted musical as you hear of them, but, wandering in the wild wastes, where man has not as yet stamped tameness upon Nature's breast, and such sounds will not seem harsh. We do not then stop to analyze, or even to particularize ; but we do realize that now we are face to face with Nature in her tragic and untamed mood, and have new impressions of the great drama that is being performed,—a drama of which many know absolutely nothing, or know through second hand, and so imperfectly. We cannot and ought not to shut our eyes and ears to tragedy, for all life has its tragic element. If we do, the world about us can never be rightly understood ; yet we need not linger long where night gathers ere the day be done, or stays in stern defiance of the sun. Happily, there is always a more cheerful path into which we may turn, a path that has only those features which go to the furthering of peace and pleasure ; where light, not shadow, greets us ; where songs of love replace the cries of exultation and despair ; where, if we desire, we may hear not alone the cheery words of my elm-tree oriole, but the gleesome rejoicing of a happy host, filling the soft summer air with " Music, good music, all day !"

I like to make positive statements, and having for more than forty years studied the ornithology of a few acres, I am a little surprised when I am contradicted; for I am frequently informed—not always politely—that some of my birds do not occur, except as migrants, in the State, and others that I class as common are rare in my locality. It would seem as if it were proper to shut our eyes to all facts that are not the facts in common possession. Doing so, how are we to increase the sum of knowledge? Rose-breasted grosbeaks are common where I live, common to the fields, the hill-side, and meadows; common even to the yard about my house. They often sing so near my open windows that the rooms are flooded with melody; inspiring music that drives our doubts to the background and fills the heart with hope. This bird does not whistle to keep his courage up, but finding his little world one more of light than shade, would have all the world to know it. It is no idle whim of an idle fellow to assert that the birds about us teach many a valuable truth, but, overestimating ourselves, we turn away, indifferent to their suggestiveness. Not at all that birds are intended to be our teachers, but he who neglects to profit by what happens before his eyes—neglecting it because not within the pale of humanity—throws away golden opportunities of bettering his life. Deaf to a bird's song, he nurses many a sorrow that he might drown, and cheats himself of the soul-refreshing pleasure of music that is more than a concourse of sweet sounds. The evening song of a thrush, recalling other days and making the present moment one of such exquisite pleasure that every care in life is for the time forgotten, lingers with us, soothing as some magic balm, when the skill of the harper and voice of the *artiste* have been quite forgotten.

To me it is marvellously strange that the world at large is so utterly indifferent to bird-life, and that governments will spend millions to protect the seals of a far-distant sea and never lift a finger to stay the destroying hand of a greedy few that profit by the slaughter of our native birds, the birds of our door-yards even, selling the skins of their victims to thoughtless women who hope to prove more attractive because of a gaudy head-gear. But what of our laws for the protection of birds? I hear you ask,—What of them, indeed? What is any law that by common consent is looked upon as a dead letter? Who ever troubles himself to enforce it, and by what a host of technicalities can it be evaded! How common, too, to find those most interested, people living in the country, content with the seductive half-knowledge due to generalization from insufficient facts, and declaring war when every condition of their material prosperity calls for peace! No birds and a plague of insects,—a plague of insects and the loss of the harvest. I would that these words were written upon every guide-post at the cross-roads and hung upon the walls of every school-house in the land.

But it is wisdom on my part to leave to other and abler hands this subject of bird protection. Perhaps I am too prejudiced in their favor. The cunning of a thieving crow so wins my admiration that I am blinded to the financial aspect of the question. There is positive pleasure in being cheated by a crow; it so effectually snubs our vanity, and we are taught that in some ways we are not lords of creation. Too often we lack due consideration and crow over our neighbors, but with good reason the crows can crow over us all. These black rascals, as they are unfairly called, often take my watermelons and I am out of pocket, but not altogether a loser. I have gained knowledge by experience and more nearly realize what a bird really is.

And a word in conclusion as to the bird-world's more popular representatives, and here again I leave their economic significance to be discussed by the professional ornithologist. I know birds better as musicians; that is from a purely personal and selfish stand-point, and speaking from such I commend to you these birds whenever you are moved to approach nearer to Nature and forget for the time being the vexations that dog your steps as careworn humanity.

Have you heard the songs at sunrise, and, too, those of a still earlier hour? Have you been thrilled by the enthusiasm that marks these carols at the birth of day? Have you joined with them, in spirit, and brought yourself to believe as they do that every bright, sunny, summer day is the brightest and best that ever blessed the world?   To do so is an excellent safeguard against pessimistic dyspepsia.   And as the day wore on, have you noted how the exultation that was so marked a feature at sunrise has given way almost to languor at noontide, but never the sweetness of the song is lost?   The soul is ever present, but in a weary body,—a body that renews its vigor as the afternoon hours pass, and every utterance is abundantly reassuring at sunset.   Bathed in the golden light of the setting sun and in the dreamy purple tints and ghost-like shadows of the gloaming, what incomparable sweetness is that of the lingering few that all reluctantly bid farewell to day!   Having listened thus, from dawn to dark, as I have so often listened, there is nothing but peace in the silence of the night that followed,—silence, soothing as the calm that rests in summer's star-lit skies.

Short Summer Days.

SHORT summer days that at sunrise give us a foretaste of autumn are days of both gladness and sadness. No longer the enervating heat, but too strongly are we reminded of the chilling breath of winter that even now is astir in the north country; but he deserves evil who persistently anticipates it. These short summer days are not mere sorry remnants of the season's fulness,—the scattered débris left by the merry throng that crowded the green world when days were long. If such were the rambler's thought, his would be a melancholy state,—the tree-tops sighing for him in a funereal way; but away with retrospection! The days are short, but merit is not lacking. The meadows yet are all ablaze with brilliant bloom; purple ironweed of matchless hue, and golden-rod that seems each year to be brighter than before; the dodder, fragments of a silken net, and rose-mallow, all are yet here to contradict us when we speak of the summer nearing its close. The great leafy banners and uplifted blossoms of the lotus have neither wilted nor turned pale. The freshness of May is everywhere. The days may be short, the birds silent, the breeze too cool for comfort, but it is not the end.

Where meadow brooks wind in and out among dense shrubbery, and this overshadowed by tall and stately oaks, we occasionally find a hazel-bush or two, and to all such as I know of I make an annual pilgrimage in September, gathering the few nuts these bushes produce. There may be many clumps of hazel-bushes I have never found. I thought I knew this region thoroughly years ago, when I was beginning to study it. I am wiser now.

No nut but is an autumn fruit, but no frost has touched here as yet, and I give no thought of what might be when I come. More than one of these clusters of hazel-bushes has acquired a summery sacredness now, and my visits are only made when I am alone. The recollections of other years must not be interrupted. At least once a year my companion returns to

Overshadowed by tall and stately oaks.

the hazels, and always on the day that I have chosen. I see him, I hear him ; we talk and shout as merrily as ever, yet my companion left me forever, oh, how long, long ago ! Had frost and storm driven all freshness and fulness from the face of Nature, it would still be summer when I gather the few hazel-nuts about which lingers the ineffaceable halo of thoughts too deep for tears. Or I wander to the lone hickories that stand like patient sentinels on the broad pastures and gather the few shellbarks that have dropped in advance of the bidding of frost. They smack of autumn, surely ; but no, there is too much freshness still remaining. The grass is too green upon which they fall, and I do not think of the end that is so near. Mankind in general seems averse to winter, unless his lot is cast in some large city, and so honestly regrets that summer so soon, as it seems to him, draws to a close. It is so, too, with those whose happier lot is cast in the country, and who, like myself, love, as my neighbors call it, to loaf. We loafers, then, disliking any marked change when the world is so suited to us, as it is, fight against the sobering thought of summer's ending and may do so successfully if we keep in certain paths, but a chance step may defeat our over-brave conclusions.   It is probable that before the day closes we will wander from the meadow to the creek-side.   If we do, the whole scene is likely to be changed and our minds changed with it.   We cannot always force ourselves to believe a fiction true, however pleasing it may be.   However riotous in the realms of fancy, we cannot always tarry there, but must walk at times soberly and in the presence of plain facts.   There are limitations even to our imaginations.   No one ever likens our autumn foliage to a flower-garden.   It is too pronounced a phase of the passing year to be compared with other phenomena, and so it was to-day when I reached the wooded shores of a sluggish, unknown creek.   At every turn I saw the scarlet lobelia, the torch that lights the footsteps of departing summer, and I knew what these shortened days meant.   It was not strange that birds were not singing, that the hum of insect life was subdued, and even the clouds were anchored in the dreamy skies.   It is the day after, with nothing but reminiscence filling each languid moment. However widely open are our eyes and ears, the gateways of the mind, we can detect nothing of the activity of days gone by. Scarlet lobelia is the bloom of all others celebrating the achievements of the past, and has only hints of a less glorious future. It is a retrospective bloom, and not, like April violets, a prophetic flower. Need we sit down by the nearest river or in the shade of a Babylonian willow and weep because of this? I never thought so. This summer is not to prove the very last, and there is more of the world still than our senses can fully comprehend. A full day is the very opposite of an overcrowded one; a day with its single, all-absorbing object overflows when one that is kaleidoscopic merely dazzles and is empty at the last. And what day but has its worthy topic, be it long or short? What though the sun sets now an hour sooner than in midsummer, it has more than enough daylight for the busiest brain. Short, indeed! But might we not more consistently worry over our own shortcomings, our many limitations, in endeavoring to encompass the significance of the shortest day? Was it mere coincidence, I wonder, when, looking from the scarlet lobelia to its reflection in the clear water beneath, I saw many glistening, silvery fishes playing about the glowing stalk of bloom, and I remembered not that they saw neither plant nor image, but as-

suming it, a bond between us was established? Let us but have some common interest with the simplest form of life, and we will realize how much the least and greatest forms of life have in common. I entered into the sports of a school of minnows so far as to be convinced that play was their object, and not some prosy effort to obtain food. I know it is denied to them, but why should not fishes have their measure of pure enjoyment? No angler of experience ever called a gamy fish a fool. That the angler fools them is not to the point. How very little we know of our common fishes beyond their anatomy; the secret of their lives from season to season has baffled our naturalists, and their history has yet to be written. Whether our present ignorance arises from indifference or the inability to overcome their cunning at concealment, I do not know, but to scoop a dozen from the water and give them long Latin names seems to have satisfied our ichthyologists to date, and yet the humblest minnow of a weedy brook can readily confound philosophers. Happily, the day of "new species" is over, but that of species new to a locality will continue to the end of time. A September ramble this year may be inch for inch as last year so far as the paths you follow are concerned, but there will not be quite the same sights and sounds. It is the certainty of this difference that makes our strolling an unfailing joy.   Only those who have had the experience can realize what a thrilling incident is the finding of a plant or animal that you have not found before.   You feel yourself one of Nature's favored ones, as if the sun was shining for you rather than your neighbor.   Even the possibility of such an occurrence or the thought of such a possibility is a sufficient incentive to take a walk.   Find a rare plant, and the shortest day will seem long because of the fulness of interest that crowds every hour.   Such a discovery starts a train of thought that is likely to tax the brain, but in a healthy way.   How came it where you found it?   Why never here before?   You may not satisfy yourself, probably will not, but the whole plant-world is clothed with greater dignity, and just a suspicion of the philosopher will cling to your skirts.

Another and more likely feature of a stroll is the finding of objects new to yourself, but familiar enough to the masters of science.   This should not lessen your pleasure one iota.   The rambler is concerned with himself and his own ignorance, and no one is so well taught as the self-taught.   Let this never be forgotten.   See with your own eyes, and having seen, be as firm concerning the fact as is the rock-ribbed earth ; but be very sure you see aright. Do not leave the spot thinking, but knowing. There is a vast difference, and time too often allows the former to merge into the latter, and your impression becomes a conviction. Such results, like poisonous snakes, are to be avoided, and yet there may be as much disaster in allowing want of self-confidence to unmake you, and the facts lose their value treating them as probabilities merely. Much has been lost to the world in consequence of this. There is no setting apart of a few men who are to be the world's fact-determiners. The wood-chopper at his work is as likely to see a rare bird as the naturalist with his gun and field-glass. He may not know that it is rare, but he does know that it is rare to him ; and woe betide the theorist who declares the wood-chopper unfamiliar with the woods. That which has been declared non-existent has too often proved prevalent when the unlearned has gained a hearing.

The arrogance of learning, defending snap judgment, is a potent cause of the continuance of ignorance.   Only recently two great names clouded their reputations by talking authoritatively of this neighborhood, which one of them has never seen and the other never studied. Scarcely a statement made was correct in any particular, but what was spoken was sent over the whole land by the public prints, and the labors of those who have bravely borne the heat and burden of exploration goes for naught.   It does not augur well for the advancement of science when men are more given to maintaining the positions they have taken on important questions than admitting they are mistaken and eager to proclaim the truth that others have discovered.   It is not strange that the masses look with some suspicion on what is called expert testimony.   Can it be that a life-long familiarity with simple conditions goes for nothing, and with Nature forever before us, we shall die without an inkling even of what has been and is now occurring before our eyes?

The shadows of the tall hickories in the smooth meadows are creeping eastward.   A purple mist is gathering along the jagged outline of the horizon, and one by one the trees that stand afar off are shut from view. Nearer it comes, and the pastures fade away, and now, as the sun sinks behind the old oaks that line the creek's wild shores, I stand alone, shut in from all the world, yet not alone. A crested tit, full of faith as to bright hours to-morrow, whistles dull melancholy to the winds and hails me as we stand by the meadow gate, bringing a cheerful message as ever, arguing, in its own sweet, persuasive way, there is always ground for happiness. Every bird is a willing teacher when we are anxious to be taught. An idle whim, perhaps, but I have long held that the crested tit is a philosopher, and insists that we be not so intent upon what is passing away that we see not that which is coming. These are short summer days, it is true, but what of the fulness of approaching autumn?

An October Outing.

OCTOBER is the charming prelude to the stern tragedy of winter. It means a clear atmosphere and colored leaves, and with them, never to be overlooked, the screaming blue-jay and the fretful crow. Better still if a red-tailed hawk sends his shrill cry down to you from the depths of the deep blue sky. Frost has dulled the golden-rod and the asters have lost their freshness, but the grass is green, and a snowy orchid on its slender stalk has a goodly array of pure, waxy flowers that seem out of place. Much remains to the rambler for which to be thankful, but the month's chief glory is the harvest of nuts. So I have always maintained, and with the regularity of a religious fanatic gone expectantly to the nut-trees to gather my share of the harvest. Strangely enough, it is the incidents of the journey to and fro that I most distinctly remember, and the goal is not prominent. To-day it rained steadily, yet I walked as usual to the shellbark hickories, gathering a harvest as I went of greater value than the nuts that whitened the closely cropped meadow. I saw many bluebirds. It is not long since I was told that the bluebird was threatened with extinction, and one more feature of the familiar meadows would soon be but a memory. It was well worth exposure to a northeast rain to see and hear these birds again. They have passed the danger line. Natural forces will not prevail against them, but what about mankind? Is it likely that boys will be allowed toy guns, and fashion call for blue feathers in bonnet decoration? The bluebirds have returned, and is not this simple statement enough to rouse interest in bird protection?

A word here concerning their encouragement. Can we cultivate them as was formerly done? My own efforts in this direction have proved of no avail against the attacks of English sparrows, but this is no reason why our ingenuity should not be further taxed. I will say this much, that the destruction of sparrows' nests in April seems to so disturb the birds that they quit the neighborhood for the summer, and if the bluebirds could be taught this fact, a step in the desired direction would be taken. How far what I have been told holds good I do not know from observation, but I am assured that gourds hung well up and so fixed that they have some motion

when perched upon will be accepted by the bluebirds and purple martens, but sparrows will not go near them, being afraid of that, to them, suspicious swaying motion. It might be thought by the snugly housed mortal that low-lying meadows of a rainy day was drawing very near to the portals of desolation, and so it is, if you take a telescopic view of them from the window next your fireside ; but drops of water are not serious obstacles to the progress of an earnest man, and what was not shunned by the bluebirds that I had no desire to shun. It makes some difference as to whom you share your discomforts with, and with birds as companions the gloomy aspects of creation are fringed with rosy light. The song of the bluebird is next in merit to the laughter of a friend, and I should fear to listen to sweeter music lest I prove to have an unappreciative ear. Then, too, absorbing attention on a single object causes us to forget that we are plagued with myriads of petty ills. I heard the bluebird, saw it, and was oblivious to all else. The clogging infirmities of increasing years rolled off my shoulders as surely as the rain-drops ; but do not, after fifty, delude yourself into jumping over ditches without previous estimate of their width. I have heard more than one man exclaim impatiently, "Oh ! I'm as young as ever," and jump, but he did not reach the opposite bank, and his day's ramble was spoiled. Exceptions occur, of course, and old John Riker, at sixty, outran a wing-tipped snipe, jumped two broad ditches, and held on to his gun while so doing ; but then he was a Dutchman who was more at home in a marsh than on a board floor. Now that I have given up running, I do not think anything is to be gained by rapid locomotion. Sour grapes? I think not. This is the same meadow, this the same bluebird, and myself, almost, the same mortal of forty years ago. What of northeast storms at such a time! My little play was more than worth the candle. And all this may continue unless fashion demands blue feathers. Let us hope the Audubon Societies will save us from the sorrow of the bluebird's extinction.

I could not stand still all the morning, and my progress drove the birds beyond my hearing, but my pleasure remained, so vivid was the recent meeting. It would have been well, perhaps, to have gone directly home and spent the day in retrospection ; for, however near to the ideal is an outing, it is sure to have a shadow lurking near its sunshine, and the brighter this the darker the other. I soon began to notice among the leafless trees and shrubbery numbers of unsuspected nests. How my pride was affected! All through the early summer I had been boasting. For once, at least, I had had eyes equal to every occasion. Nothing had escaped me, and now, following a daily trodden path, and sometimes at arm's length, I find empty nests, and some of them of birds that I must have overlooked. How little the field naturalist really knows in comparison with what it is possible to know! The past summer was the most bird-full I have ever known, and every nest I discovered fired my ambition to find still another and another, and I hunted until the field was exhausted Exhausted? Here are several that I did not find when they were occupied. Nature issues no bulletins for man's benefit, and the man is not yet born who can keep track of her activities. Seeing a little, we think that little all. It must be remembered, too, that many nests are so slightly constructed that they fall to pieces before the onset of brisk autumnal gales. The many nests that I found some months ago were but a fraction of what were built here on the home meadows; and what of the broad acres of my several neighbors? I have never seen a spot that reached to perfection, in my mind, but soon I found that another spot excelled it. The Crosswicks marshes have been called a birds' paradise, but there are hundreds of equally paradisiacal areas not far off, and only the shadow of man's carelessness prevents the sunshine of perfection being realized. Too many cry out impatiently, Who cares for a chippy-bird? And the result is the keeping back of the hand that could prevent the birds' destruction. He who cries, Who cares? is the world's worst enemy.

The bluebirds came back when I reached the hickories, and sang as I gathered the scattered nuts,—a song for every nut I gathered, so it seemed; and the pitiless rain was quite forgotten. When the serious labor of the day was over, the economic purpose of the outing accomplished, I turned again to the birds, but they had gone. This is no unusual experience. The song remains so distinctly that we do not mark the withdrawal of the singer. When this happens, we have reached the flood-tide of appreciation, the high-water mark of our capability to realize what a bird's song really is.

The Crosswicks marshes.

He has deaf ears who finds it only a pleasant but unsuggestive sound. As we draw a circle to represent our globe, so a single note of a bluebird tells me the story of the round year. It is again spring, with all that the season of promise means to us; it is again summer, with earth's goodliest gifts before us; it is autumn, rich with ripened fruit and brilliant color; it is winter, only dreary to those who know not what this season means. If danger still exists, let Audubon Societies everywhere come to the bluebird's rescue. We never exhaust a locality, however frequently we pass through it, yet, strangely enough, we assume this on our return from the outermost limit of our walls. Everything happens, so it is recorded in the books, when going out; nothing when coming in. This really means that we are wearied of sightseeing by the middle of the day, and long for an afternoon nap. We lose about one-half of our possibilities by giving way to a desire to return. Expend all your energy in locomotion, and the world is two blank walls, between which you hurry. You can narrow the widest meadow until it is little better than a prison cell. All that is needed is to keep your eyes in the direction of home and close your ears to the birds about you. Not overburdened with the nuts I had picked up, and with less rain to annoy, I attempted cataloguing the newly found empty nests, and found still others. Here was severe snubbing, for I have always been proud of my powers of observation. I must have mistaken for a spider's web, heavy with dust, a nest of a little flycatcher, and a downy woodpecker must have been mottled lichen only when it was cutting out a brand-new nest in a little tree. Where were all the cat-birds when I was here in June? I trust to having my eyes more widely open in the coming year, and my ears more quick to catch each passing note. I have said this before. But if humiliating to take a walk in October, it is also instructive. A careful study of empty nests in leafless trees will teach us how to look and where to look when the nest-building season comes again, and no one has yet determined just how far old nests are utilized in the construction of new ones. I have known a new nest to be built within three feet of one of the preceding year, and I am positive not a twig of the latter was taken away; but old nests are not always left to gradually fall apart and disappear. The pretty white-footed mouse will rebuild or refit a cat-bird's nest and have a snug home that defies the winter's storms; but an even more entertaining instance of reoccupation is when a big gray spider lines with web a chipping-sparrow's nest, and builds from it a gauzy approach. One that I found to-day had a veranda, a lawn of gossamer, "all and singular" the features of any home of man, or even moated castle of other days and lands. In no other ways do I recall the utilization of old birds'-nests, but, even if deserted by every living creature, they never lose their suggestiveness until bit by bit they have been scattered by the winds.

It is folly to spoil the day by wondering and worrying about what has not been seen. Let the restful hours of the evening, after an outing, be given to the better realization of what has been observed. That is only half seen upon which the eyes merely rested. Sitting to-night by the open fire, I have only to hold before me a single hickory-nut, and the old trees, the meadows, and the path leading thereto are all before me, and I see with a clearer vision and renewed delight that which has been before me daily for these many years.

These many years! There could not be a more unfortunate phrase come to mind, unless we desire to invite blue devils. Every hero of my childhood has passed away and I am classed among old folks. It is hard to realize, and out of doors I quite forget it. Not so before the open fire. Every flame is the epitome of an ill-spent year. Every sudden brightening of the room as a clearer light springs from the fireplace is to me the vivid recollection of blundering days. It is so easy, afterwards, to see where we were groping and stumbling in the dark, and why. Light and the need of it do not always walk hand in hand. The glowing backlog is one long panorama of the past, and why the pleasures of other days keep in the background is a puzzle to me. I cannot force them into prominence. Blue devils have the upper hand to-night, and have had these many years.

These many years! The victim of blue devils is a willing one. I will be gay to-night in spite of them. Fresh fuel may fright them from my little room. Many are the big chunks —I like this word "chunk," though it finds scant welcome in the dictionary—big chunks of knotty wood that my neighbors had allowed to remain wheresoever chance had put them that I have gathered and gloried in when they crowned the pile of fagots in the fireplace, and towered above the slender brass posts of the andirons,—household fixtures that link me to colonial days. It is all very well for Americans to sniff at genealogical research, as a good many do, and affect indifference to the facts of their family history, but just so far I am un-American, if you choose, for I do care a great deal, and am more proud of the fact that I can sit before grandmother's andirons than if I had sold an essay and bought a new pair. A pleasant thought is an enviable possession, and I have many such when facing the open fire. Andirons now play a new part; they are finger-posts directing backward to days when the axe was more important among tools than it is to-day; for a hatchet will suffice among saplings. What of the skilled wood-choppers of other days ?   There are none left in this neighborhood ; their ashes are mingled with those of the forest.   Anybody can hack a tree down, if he keeps long enough at it, but to skilfully fell an old chestnut is another matter ; cut and split it to posts, rails, fire-wood, and fagots ; putting every bit of it to some use and leaving a level-topped stump upon which you might set the dishes for your supper.   This is a lost art ; irrecoverable perhaps as the marvellous tales the woodmen of the last century told to the children of that day. I wonder how much of all they told was true. Very little, possibly ; very much, probably ; for it is hard to even imagine how a primeval forest and its belongings could be exaggerated.

The chunk upon the andirons to-night is from somewhere up the river, brought down by the last freshet and left, very conveniently, on my meadows.   There is on it a curious ring-like growth, the attempt to heal over where a branch has died and dropped off.   An opening has been left, and looks so smooth at one point, I fancy squirrels have been passing to and fro for many generations.   My chunk is part of an old tree, that perhaps, after standing long near the river-shore, was cut down at last to make room for improvements! Strange as it may seem, I have known an old tree to be cut down because the vacant space was considered an improvement. If the lower animals had been such fools as some men are, evolution would never have reached to the human species. If trees, when burning, would only sing a swan-song as they turn to ashes! Something akin to this once happened. I placed a gnarly root on the fire, and while watching, in a dreamy way, the flames play about it, there was a sudden snapping and hissing that roused me, and just in time. The root at one point opened and untwisted and a dull gray object was exposed. Warped, blackened, and gaping wide, it proved to be a pewter snuff-box, in which was a many-folded paper. This defied all my efforts to save it; but I have the box still, and how often I have wondered as to its history! What a splendid basis for a story might have been recorded on that folded paper, for it was covered with writing!

The world is welcome to anthracite or cannel glowing in the cheerful grate,—give me my andirons and a chunk of wood.

A Northeast Storm.

Why raindrops should fall in a very disagreeable manner is not apparent. Their single purpose is to reach the ground, we presume, but, as in many another case where the operations of Nature are concerned, do we not presume too much? Whether or not, northeast raindrops are as different from those of a summer shower as sand from swan's-down. To-day a northeast storm prevails, and to study its peculiarities is a serious undertaking, as every attractive feature of merely falling water has been eliminated. In short, we are brought face to face with tragedy, and I would, influenced wholly by my own taste, that there was less of it in the world, in our lives, and in literature. Especially do I dislike to be brought face to face with death and disaster when I settle down before the cheerful fire on the andirons and open a new book. There is more than sufficient of both entering into our daily walks to satisfy us, and to make sure of comfort I want to be moved to laughter, not to tears. No one laughs, it is supposed, when facing a northeast storm, and in November, too, when every expression of these melancholy days is given a rising inflection, is emphasized with energy, and not a puff of rain-burdened wind but whispers " Fool !" as you pass onward. Why I ever deliberately go out of doors and face such stormy weather is not to be explained, at least by me. I go, but I do not know why. I invariably wish that I had not gone, but never turn back until some reasonably distant goal is reached. I do not see much, for every living creature takes shelter now as it never does at any other time. You see but few birds, and these not willing wanderers, and I believe I never overtake a meadow-mouse or catch an out-door opossum or squirrel. Other people sometimes do, of course. All the world is more fortunate than myself, but a northeast storm is my synonyme for forsaken fields. The air, now, seems too full of water to hold anything else, and such a wail of utter hopelessness comes from the twiggy tops of the beeches and old oaks when the wind with fitful fierceness rushes through them. This dismal moaning is enough of itself to drive all wild life to close cover, and it seems to do so. Solitary crows, that folk-lore says betoken sorrow, are the storm's most fitting attendants,—single crows that fly moodily with the wind and never utter a sound as they pass by. I was prepared to see this forlorn creature beating its way over the fields, at times swooping down as if it would clutch the earth and shake it, and then rising petulantly above the trees as if to be beyond reach of its old home and stamping-grounds.

Every other bird, I supposed, was snugly housed, but herein I was mistaken, which fact makes this my most memorable storm. It would appear that some, at least, of our many kinds of sparrows do not lose their appetites in any weather, and where, to-day, the weeds were rankest, there I found these birds, running like mice along the ground, but with no marked curtailment of flight power because of the driving rain. They knew very well what prolonged exposure meant, and so only flew when necessity required it. I was both right and wrong. They had sought shelter, yet not where the search for food was impracticable, and while not fearing the rain took care not to be entrapped by it. Feathers sometimes prove a leaky roof. But I could not stand long to catch uncertain glimpses of mouse-like sparrows. It is well to keep moving when out in the rain; the buffeting of the storm falls less heavily, and birds in wet weather are not peculiarly entertaining. They exhibit no new feature of their many-sided characters, and keep their familiar pleasantries as closely shut as their feathers. As much as butterflies, birds belong to sunshine and the rosy sunrise hours of our days. We think of them when flowers bloom and trees are in full leaf. We are not logical in so doing, to be sure; but then logic and a May morning are ill-suited companions. Young people, I have heard, fall in love in May, and where is logic? Too often retired to shady groves to weep. A truly philosophical state of mind leads to seeking out the reason of the discomforts of a northeast storm and not merely endeavoring to avoid them. And the discomforts, as we call them, are they such to all animal life? A bedraggled, rain-soaked mouse is a forlorn object in our sight. We suppose the creature feels our discomforts under such conditions, but does it really? One red and black woolly caterpillar kept on its course, twisting in and out among little pools of water, and did not seem affected by the pelting of rain-drops to which it was exposed ; but possibly it was muttering to itself as it went along ; growling as much as I did. How next to nothing we know of the mental status of the varied forms of life that daily cross our paths ! Indeed, can we safely say that we know anything ; is it not all inference on our part?

If only moved to the latter, why not cut the Gordian knot by remaining in-doors ? I write this for the benefit of those who shudder at the mention of a pitiless, cold, driving rain-storm, when every sound is to them a sob and every sudden increase of energy on the part of the wind is accompanied by a piercing shriek or wail of despair. That something of this is a figment of fancy, nourished in ignorance, is certainly true. Not that Nature cannot be serious and deal destruction with a lavish hand ; but, in

very truth, a northeast storm is not, or very seldom, indeed, found to be much more serious a
matter than when woman turns man's comfort
out of doors and him along with it, when clean-
ing house. That is an abomination, comparable
only to a Western blizzard or some huge tidal
wave of the Pacific. But, happily, just as the
newly cleaned house has a freshness about it
that the most crabbed old bachelor is forced to
admit, so Nature wears a fresher face and the air
is clearer, as with the last drops of the dismal
storm comes a brightening of the western sky
as the day closes. Even in November this is
an hour to be remembered,—an hour of brilliant color, of bird song, of general rejoicing.
Even the naked trees shake their gaunt sides
and exult that the northeast wind is a thing of
the past and restful quiet is now at hand,—the
quiet and comfort of drowsy, hazy sunshine,
where the greatest voluntary effort is to dream
of the many gains and few losses of the departed summer. It is worth being all day out
of doors,—yet at the time I never think so,—
however violent the storm, that we may be in
at its death and mark the progress of the new

order. The gentle, assuring breeze from the west; the splendor of the sunset, painting and gilding every broken cloud; the melody of the brave birds that sing now on their way to their roosting trees; the deepening of the shadows; the fading out of every trace of day; the solitary glory of the evening star; the rising of the moon and reillumination of the earth and sky,—these, in quick succession, follow in the track of the storm, and gladness fills the world that but a few hours before was desolate beyond endurance. No, not quite that, for however wild the storm we come out of it unscathed. We think recklessly when it rains and talk extravagantly of another deluge, but why has never been explained. As my journals for many years attest, I have faced more than a hundred northeast storms and am yet alive. Just as I called myself a fool at the outset, shivering and forlorn as I faced the wind and rain, now that it is all a thing of the past, I have no regrets and call myself fortunate. The western sky is one vast sheet of brilliant color. Warm reds and summery green extend over half the heavens. Every rain-drop clinging to the scattered leaves adds its mite to the sparkling outlook, and before me an alder, berry-laden, glows with a ruddy glow that pales even the sunset. It is to me the last outreaching flame, darting defiantly from the ashes of the dead summer.

In Defence of Desolation.

"HOW desolate!" Such is the common remark when in late autumn or winter we look
out of the window on a dull, cloudy, or possibly
rainy day. Is the asserted desolation real or
apparent? To test the merits of a locality,
choose the most hopelessly commonplace corner, some unreclaimed swampy bit that has defied the farmer, and, if it proves too full of
interest to be exhausted in one day's study,
where is the asserted desolation? The fault is
with ourselves, not with irreclaimable Nature.
We have persistently turned our backs upon
her, and so devoutly worshipped the artificial
that much of what is thoroughly good and
wholesome is looked upon with dread or indifference. The pleasure asserted of the pathless
woods is also in the trackless swamps, and lurks
in the weedy corners of badly cultivated fields.
To the untrained eye a clump of bushes may

170

be as aimlessly grouped as my neighbor's wood-
pile ; but it is not so.   There is no lack of purpose, no neglect on Nature's part, and nothing
of weed or bush or sapling that has not a
deeper significance than one is likely to fathom.
To speak of desolation because green leaves

are lacking is the arrogant speech of ignorance.
The truth is, without regard to evergreen trees,
the absence of green leaves is comparative, not
absolute.   I have not yet, in forty years' wanderings, been unable to find at least one fresh,
living leaf in the course of a morning's ramble.

Nature keeps up a sort of guerilla warfare with winter long after her main army has been defeated, and brave weeds find safe retreats and flourish unmolested in neglected nooks to which attention is never directed ; and so, casting a careless glance over the fields and forest, we exclaim, in our ignorance, how desolate !

The million lances of the thistle may avail nothing against the legions of frost ; but it would not seem so, for here, long after the grass is wilted and brown, a blooming thistle lifts its purple plumes and invites the goldfinch, now in late autumn, just as it did in the steamy hot sunny August afternoons. This is an encouragement surely to go deeper into the asserted desolation of the day. The goldfinch is no stranger even in midwinter, but when Christmas is not far off you do not expect to find him on a blooming thistle ; yet one was thus found to-day, in mid-November.

Perhaps it was when the glaciers still rested on our nearest hill-sides that the ancestral crested tit looked out upon the sunshine of a bright May morning, and in the exuberance of its joy whistled, *Sweet here.* Whatever the truth, this prince of cheerfulness has never changed its tune, and no storm, not even midwinter's greatest effort, ever shut out the sunshine in this wee bird's heart. It never admits the supremacy of gloom, and finds beauty and content when we are mourning over the desolation wrought by frost. Not even the forest, now gloomier than the field, is too dreary for him, and that assuring *Sweet here* was not mockery, but a light-giving song that lifted the cloud.

There is no other bird that has the same awakening power. To-day the cardinal, that has for a time been silent and moping in the denser underbrush, came from his hiding, echoed the tit's emphatic words, and added many another. " Clouds and bare branches do not ruin the world" is the theme of his November song, and what the hill-side lacks in sunshine is made good by the brilliant glow of his crimson coat. He is a pessimist indeed who can find the world askew when such birds are singing.

I had not passed through the garden before I had seen and heard three singing birds, and now at the stile I was greeted by the Carolina wren. If possible, it was more desolate under

the old oaks than in the meadows, for the leafless branches are so many and interlaced, they
shut out the light. On a dark day, to go into
the woods is like passing from the gloaming to
night; yet here, facing a forbidding east wind,
the Carolina wren was singing. Not humming
to itself to rouse the memory of brighter days,
but a whole-souled declaration of content, though
the sky was gray and an east wind muttered
vengeance as it hurried by. I hear this bird all
the year through. It is my daily companion,
and never a thought of desolation when it is
singing at my elbow. There is no desolation.
Looking at the world from the library window,
seeing nothing and hearing less, what right have
we to be so critical of Nature's methods? The
browns of autumn make the greens of spring
less tiresome, and when many birds, or even one,
can be as cheerful as a Carolina wren, although
every feature of the day be forbidding, why
should mankind declaim against the desolation
of the outlook? It is infinitely better to be
warmed by the assuring songs of a bird than to
hover over the register of a stuffy room. November fogs, east winds, clouded skies! Go

out and hear what the birds say of them, and you will find the world less black than you had painted it.

Even the little brown tree-creeper does not feel necessitated to keep on the leeward side of the tree-trunks, though wind and snow and even hail conspire to dislodge it. It squeaks its satisfaction, and while it held on, though a stiff breeze was blowing, I saw the plucky bird draw a worm from a cranny in the bark : swallowing its prey, it snapped its beady eyes at me and squeaked a suggestive "Good-morning" as it hurried away. That bird never missed the sunshine. The day was not so bad that it might not be worse ; and if birds are satisfied, why not ourselves ?

A dead tree, stricken in its prime by lightning, is as nearly typical of desolation as any object I have ever seen. I will never believe that such things ought to be. But the dead and decaying hickory gave rise to fewer gloomy thoughts when a woodpecker came and beat in a rhythmic way that was akin to music. Mere noise, perhaps you insist ; but there is method in it, something lacking at times in in-door chatter.

A red-headed woodpecker in November, and cloudy at that, is equal to half a dozen sunbeams. It will penetrate the gloom to that extent, and send desolation a little deeper into the beyond.

Six birds already, and my walk has just commenced. There is yet a trace of youthful vigor left. I always jump from the top step of the stile; not always gracefully, I admit; and, tripping this time, I shook the near earth as I sprawled in the briers. Bob White went off with a whirr as if I was some blundering sportsman; and I had not picked a tenth of the desmodium and bidens seeds from my clothing before another and another went whizzing off to my neighbor's sproutland, whither I too was bound. Could a field in November be suddenly shorn of its weeds, what a wealth of wild life would be exposed! Looking across country, it is by mere chance we see any bird, and very seldom life of any other form. Birds can see us when we cannot see them; probably, while I was yet several rods away, a skulking woodcock knew of my approach. Quail and woodcock! I did not smack my lips over them as mere "gobbets of venison," but snapped my eyes thankfully at them for aiding so materially in disproving the assertion that cloudy, storm-threatening autumn days are desolate.

The day was darkening, but I was not deterred. Turning towards the marshy meadows, I startled a whippoorwill, some straggler, lingering a full two months after all his brethren had sought the sunnier climes of the Gulf States; but let no straggling, over-staying bird surprise you. As I know from careful examination, insect life has not been lacking until now, and if it was a matter of food only, there has been no reason why all our whippoorwills should not have eaten their Thanksgiving dinners with us.

On the wide stretch of marshy meadows the outlook is at first forbidding, more so than on the upland fields or the wooded hill-side; but it is necessary only to accommodate oneself to the new surroundings to be assured that chaos has not come again because of your standing on a marshy meadow, with threatening clouds overhead and a fierce east wind blowing. It is Nature in a savage mood, but this has naught to do with desolation. I gave no further heed to

the conditions in general when I saw, still intact, a massive globular nest of the marsh-wren.
It is too late for the birds themselves, for they
have no liking for Nature under the new order
of things, when frost is stage manager.

You stand in such dreary places as a marshy
meadow, and wonder why you came. With only
dead vegetation about you, it is not strange ;
but such feelings vanish when one by one the
lurking life begins to grow restive, and your attention is called, now this way, now that; to the
pool in the marsh in front of you, to the tangle of wilted rose-mallow or great, gray, wilted
leaves of the classic lotus at one side, or to the
leaden sky above that seems so low down you
are oppressed by its nearness. A marsh-owl
with a mouse in its talons may rise up as silently
as any ghost at midnight, and, alighting on
some projecting stake, proceed to devour it,
quite unconcerned by your presence. At least,
this may happen if you are equal to standing
as rigidly as a fence-post ; and this is not so
very difficult if your attention is drawn to any
occurrence that interests you. The day being
dark, it is possible that the barn-owl, living in

the cavernous hollow of an old tree, may be tempted to come out,—and a splendid fellow he is ; or if not abroad, he may be sitting at the doorway of his home, enjoying the sunless prospect, and thankful that the glaring sunshine is this day spared him.   If not so fortunate as to see this noble owl, he can be searched for and routed out, if adventure so far moves you ; but this I never advise.

Owls seem nearer to Nature than do other birds.   There is an air of mystery about them that rouses our interest.   We ask ourselves more questions when brought face to face with an owl than we do in the case of any other bird. Theirs is no meaningless stare.   They can look us out of countenance, and put as much intelligence into their eyes as we can in ours.

There is some reason for calling the owl the bird of wisdom ; and yet there is cause for wondering if the crow is not mentally his superior.   Crows are not disheartened by the gloom of late autumn.   If the fog is too dense to fly through it, they rise above it or trot about the ground, discussing the situation with their fellows.   Is this speaking too positively?   I have long been familiar with an observing man who has lived all his days within sight and hearing of crows. He claims to understand their language, and can repeat the "words" that make up their vocabulary. Certainly crows seem to talk; but do they? Does a certain sound made by them have always the one significance? Year after year I have listened and watched, watched and listened, and wondered if my friend was right. He believes it. I believe it almost. Are there limitations to ornithological interpretation? And is this an instance where truth is unattainable? We know that crows are cunning, and by their mother wit have withstood the persecutions of mankind; we know that they have a wide range of utterances, and not one is put forth merely to gratify the ear, as in the case of a thrush's song; yet we hesitate to say plainly that crow talketh unto crow and that they take counsel together. There is no physical or metaphysical reason why this should not be the case; there is abundant evidence pointing in that direction, but no actual demonstration, satisfying every one, has taken place. Were we less theory-ridden and more observant, the question would have been settled before this.   In such a case, the opinion of the farmer is worth more than that of the professional ornithologist.

A crow, black as night, might seem a fitting accompaniment of a dreary day and desolate outlook ; but what of the great flocks of rusty grakles and of cow-birds?   Neither is really black, but both appear so as they rise from the marsh and drift like dead leaves before the wind, perhaps to sink out of sight in the dead grass, or, gathering in the near-by trees, chirp, splutter, and gurgle in a strange yet not un-musical way.   These are northern grakles that are now southward bound, and quite different from their purple, boat-tailed cousins that were here all summer.   The cow-birds are not migra-tory, strictly speaking, but will come and go all through the winter ;—curious birds, uncertain in all their ways, and fitting into no scheme of well-regulated communities.   Building no nests and never mating, what can we expect of them ? Yet their presence to-day is more than welcome. However desolate in appearance, the world is not deserted.

Without moving from the spot at which I have been standing this half-hour, by a mere upraising of my eyes I can see an eagle perched on the tall dead sassafras near the river-shore ; a black hawk nearer by, intent upon the shallow waters directly beneath where it is perched ; and a broad-winged buzzard, hovering over a hassock where a meadow-mouse is lurking, helpless perhaps from fear, knowing well the enemy that is so swift and sure when it does strike. But not every swooping falcon rises from the earth with prey. The dim light of a cloudy November afternoon might be some excuse for failure, but even when light and wind and all else is favorable, it is never so much as fifty out of a possible hundred. Many a time I have seen a hawk pounce and pounce again, and then fly away with a shrill scream, clearly indicative of its intense disgust.

The frost and thin ice at times have driven away much of the bird-life of these wide-spread marshes. The redwings have gone, the reed-birds disappeared, and the swamp-sparrows have wandered to more sheltered spots, but the reeds and cat-tail are not deserted. If we watch the bared areas of mud, now that it is low tide, we will surely see the common sora, or rail, and not improbably the Virginia rail. Occasionally the latter remains all winter, and the sora is often forced to do so because of slight gun-shot wounds that prevent migration ; but such birds do not, I think, survive the winter. Many are caught by the hawks, and some fall victims to the sly snapping-turtle and to pike, before the general freeze-up ; others succumb to intense cold.

What I have warrant to expect seeing, before the day is done, is the great blue heron ; and to start up the delicate least bittern is not improbable. The heron is not shy, and too big, one might think, to conceal itself, yet it can stand motionless among sticks and grass, quite invisible to any but a well-trained eye. Taking up a new position, as I supposed, I flush a heron from the willow hedge : how the big bird brightens the landscape ! It utters no wild yawp, as if badly frightened, but moves easily at a slight elevation, and would again alight, but something again disturbs it, and now it rises into the upper air by a few rapid and very vigorous wing-strokes. Its long legs no longer are an encumbrance, as they at first appear to be, but are fixed in an outreaching position and offer no resistance to the bird's progress. The old days of the peregrine falcon are no more, and the bird here has no enemies. The bald eagle that was recently in sight might prove a dangerous foe were it so disposed, but it cares for fish and mammals more than birds, and I have never seen one attack a heron or any bird on these meadows. Negative evidence, of course, and of less significance because eagles are rare now, and herons not so abundant as forty years ago. The indifference of farmers, and that abuse of freedom, allowing anybody and everybody to carry a gun at all seasons, has done its deadly work. Where there should be a hundred birds we are fortunate now if we see ten. Time was when there were herons and heronries and stately white egrets along the river-shore, and the creeks teemed with wild fowl in season. It is a cause to be thankful, to-day, that the heron, a single heron, has given to this dismal day the charm of its presence, and so added to the evidence that the exclamation, "How desolate !" was not merited.

I grant that deserted Nature may be desolate. An arid desert, with no life upon it except scorpions and spiders, may be the climax of desolation ; but no such conditions obtain here. Even if the storms, with all possible accessories of discomfort, beat upon us, there is a resisting energy in the wild life that has wisely chosen these marshes as its home. Discomfort for the day is far removed from desolation ; and if you persist in calling it such, then let me argue in its defence. Dark, dismal days, such as this, are really pleasing by way of variety. Already I have seen many birds, when the outlook from the hill-top was anything but assuring ; but then there was the goldfinch almost at my door, and the crested tit announcing " All's right !" before I had gone a dozen rods. Through the window, desolate, perhaps ; but what of a closer inspection ? It is ever so.

There is yet an hour before sunset, but no ruddy light will illuminate the wide-reaching marsh. Night will quickly come, but here is the winding creek, forsaken now by trapper and fisherman. The wind foretells the rain in no uncertain terms, and even these hardy men care much for the comforts of a shelter. They know that the autumn flight of wild-fowl has taken place. They know that the little pools and winding brooks that drain the meadows are likely to be visited by pintail ducks and widgeon, and that now the home-bred summer ducks are hobnobbing in the marsh with their cousins from the up-country. The gunner knows this, but it is going to rain, and not for ducks will he get wet. They will not pass away with the storm, he thinks.

Perhaps not, but I will not risk it. The greater my triumph, the more I see, and so prove the day not empty, the country not desolate. Here, as I expected, I startle widgeon from the wilted cat-tails, and the pintail ducks, taking warning, rise with a clatter into the air, without knowing what the danger may be. They are all gone, and the cold, glittering reaches of old Crosswicks are forbidding. The storm is too near for comfort I admit, yet sight-seeing is not at an end. Almost at my feet, as I stand on the bank of the little river, is a coot that floats as lightly as a cork, and holds its head as erect as a June rose in the sunshine.

The world is not wrong with it.   If the waters are a bit troubled by the wind, a little more care is needed perhaps ; but what of that?   Its feathers are comparatively storm-proof, and there is always quiet underneath the waves. The commotion made life merrier for the coot, as a bit of excitement adds a healthy pulse-beat to our sluggish selves.

But I must hurry away : the darkness means a great deal if it overtakes you on the marsh. I give another searching glance at the wind-tossed water as I turn from it.   There, for the first, I see a little brown dab-chick, a distant cousin of the coot's, and just as happy as that strange bird.   It dived as I saw it, but immediately reappeared, and I waved it a good-by.

I might have accepted my friend's dictum, moped in front of the andirons, and believed the world desolate.   How unfair would I then have proved to myself and to the commonplace corner in which my lot is cast !   A cloudy sky, a cold east wind, a chill that reaches to the bone, and patches of moisture-laden fog may all be present ; the leafless trees may look all forlorn and not a sound reach you as you look

from the window ; but plunge into these elements of discomfort, accept no other than
your impressions after close contact, and you
will be moved to admit that only upon the
failure of a thousand happenings, and a deeper
blackness settling over the outlook than ever
did, will you be justified in exclaiming, even as
you survey the world from a window, " How
desolate !"

A Very Old Milestone.

ALMOST in the middle of a neglected field, mottled with parti-colored pebbles in winter and green during summer, when the dewberry vines run riot over the glacial drift,—here, half a mile from any public road, I recently unearthed a very old milestone, when and by whom set up nobody living knew. A knowledge of it came to me as an Indian idol, and so it was hunted up, the frozen earth removed, and the relic recovered. Closer examination proved it to be a flat, frost-split slab of slaty stone, with S. M. still decipherable upon one side, and a few dents and short lines that I cannot demonstrate ever meant anything. In proportion to their ignorance, the idle element of the neighborhood, standing about, assumed to be proficient in antiquarian lore, and took it unkindly when called fools. Had I been blind I might have imagined the ghosts of the colonists of

two centuries ago were all babbling at once.
The poor old resurrected milestone had no
chance to be heard where it was, so I took it
home, and am thankful that my door-yard is far
too wide for the neighbors to look across it.
Here both the milestone and myself are resting in peace, the latter standing boldly out in
the winter sunshine, and now a milestone once
more, but only indicating how far in the distant
past is the old township of Nottingham of two
centuries ago.

First, the Indian trail, and how long every
journey must have seemed when threading the
deep, dark woods from which dangerous foes
might at any time appear! for these were the
days of the lurking cougar, the most dangerous
of animals since the time when the Ice Age
hunter contended vainly with angered masto-
dons.   The references to the cougar in colonial
documents are few and unsatisfactory, yet these
fierce creatures lingered here long after Euro-
pean occupation of the country, and certainly
before then were not rare, if we may judge
from the traces of them found in the ashes of
the earlier Indian village sites.   Among these

I recall a curiously fashioned fragment of a lower jaw, with the teeth in place, the purpose evidently being that of an ornament. Teeth and claws of bears are still popular with the untamed red man, and this bit of a cougar's jaw told the same story. I have seen, too, a rude etching on a slate that seemed to be intended for this animal,—one of the few inscribed stones which could not be held in suspicion, not passing through too many hands before reaching an archæologist.

Peter Kalm makes no reference to the cougar, and yet it was still roaming through South Jersey even at the time of his visit, 1749, but, presumably, of rare occurrence.

After the trail, a bridle-path, or, more correctly, the one became the other, through the same boundless forest, extending as it did from the river to the ocean. It was available, as a path, for a horse and its rider only, and some years elapsed before it was widened and became a roadway for carts. Here documentary evidence helps us a little. The cart-road in time became a highway that permitted the use of four-wheeled vehicles, but it was still a twisting, turning, serpentine route, following the same lines that the Indians had found, those of least resistance to foot travel.   Then came the new, direct roads from town to town, and the approximately geometric marking of farm boundaries.   From the Indian trail to the bicycle-

path seems an indefinitely long time, but there are people living who have seen one-half of it. My recovered milestone faced the storms, but saw little of the sunshine of more than one-half of the last two centuries.   The forest was too dense for even summer sunbeams to penetrate.

It is a little difficult to realize now, when practically all the one-time natural features of the region have been removed, that our public roads, as they now are, did not spring at once into existence at the command of the surveyor. Some of them did, but the main thoroughfares, the old-time roads, grew into being very gradually, and, time-honored, should not their old name of "road" be retained? What sickly sentimentality that changes it to "avenue," as we find the case in many a city! Now, the pedestrian's highway is the winding foot-path along the hill-side, with an old worm-fence on one side and a respectable wood on the other. This is the squirrel's and chipmunk's highway also, so one is pretty sure of lively company, or if this is too remote, the pedestrian can take the "back road," or that most remote from the popular lines of travel; a deep sandy road that defies the bicycle and so leaves the foot-passenger happy. May such roads long continue! Pay the supervisor his salary, but pray him not to earn it. If only as a prostrate monument to good old times, let us have here and there a road such as suited our easy-going grandfathers. Nature, when unmolested, does not unmake a road, but puts many a finishing touch upon it, and happy is the traveller who passes that way. When such roads go out of existence, walking will become mere locomotion and the pedestrian by choice a curiosity. The whirling throng of to-day that glory in wheeling-paths and macadam are becoming familiar enough with the wayside halting-places of their rapid transits, but what of the intermediate country? No spot quite empty to the eager-eyed, and life lurks in many a tangle just over the fence. The weeds of a single summer's growth can effectually conceal the largest bird or beast that is now found in our country; ay, that has been found here since the days of the mastodon and giant elk. I found weeds, not long since, that were eight feet high; but then, who cares for weeds?—is not the very name one of reproach? and such foul growths are to be shunned, not sought. Until fools are dead this will ever be the case; but a wilderness of weeds of a single summer's growth will well repay most careful exploration. It can offer stout resistance to your progress, and what may not hyssop and boneset and iron-weed and dudder conceal? Your legs and arms held fast by the Gordian knot of greenbrier, you magnify, when helpless, every unexplained condition, and a foot-long garter-snake will give you a passing vision of a boa-constrictor, and mice will grow to wild-cats, before you see them scampering across your feet. If you would rid the day of possible monotony, push through a pathless thicket in the corner of some neglected field ; get scratched and pricked, and warmed by the effort, if not excitement, and believe ever after that the well-known country, as you thought it, is not so well known after all. Too seldom do we leave the beaten path and leap over the farmers' fences.

Roads or paths alike are mere conveniences. We do not live on them. The little poetry they possessed passed with the times that were. Endless the stream of traffic and of pleasure it may be that now is passing to and fro, but how prosy the present when the milestone calls up a vision of the past, when the winding way through the woods was the spot where the colonists occasionally met and held earnest conversation, or, better yet, by chance young people came by, and how vividly the youth stands out in one's imagination as he leans nervously against the old stone and murmurs little nothings that elicit a scarcely audible reply !

The old milestone is intricately seamed, and many the deep lines here and there, but Nature has been the etcher. In vain has been my search for hearts transfixed by arrows ; yet in the century and more that passed when this was in very fact a milestone, some such comedy must have been acted within the reach of its noontide shadow.

S. M. stood for Stacy's Mill, and that was three miles away as the crow flies, but all traces of the figures indicating this fact have crumbled to dust. Indeed, I have but the ghost of a milestone, but ghosts are suggestive, if not lo-quacious, and how glorious it would be if many people we know were only ghosts ! Mahlon Stacy, the proprietor, had five daughters I know of, and perhaps there were others, and how un-likely that this milestone should not have been passed and repassed by anxious, meditative swains, going, of course, to the mill on business, but coming from it dissatisfied if Ruth or Rebecca had not been in evidence. In such way fancy runs wild as I look at the stone, and in more sober moments I am forced to confess the thing itself is not suggestive. How utterly stupid is a modern milestone! and why, after all, should one that has crumbled under Time's destroying touch be more so? It fails, to my sorrow, to conjure up a lengthy panorama of Colonial days. Perhaps it is as well; for if the whole truth were told our enthusiasm might be chilled. As it is, we forget that then as now there was an ugly, seamy underside of things, and the early settlers were quite as human as their successors of to-day. No; in digging up an old milestone I did not dig up a treasure. Fancy no more clings to it than water to the feathers of a duck. But I have been impatient. Looking at it again to-day, while the storm was raging, the old milestone, to my surprise, was clothed with interest. Brave snow-birds perched upon it. How suggestive they proved to be! A strange light seemed to rest upon the stone, and I saw, as in a picture, the forests of other days; and not a tree but was the resting-place of a bird. Every bush was the home of a songster, and through the grass ran the wary mother grouse and quail, with timid, peeping brood. What days were those, when their one great enemy had not appeared in force, civilized, cultured, charitable, tender-hearted man ! The milestone brought a vision to me of the day when this foe to the bird world had not yet asserted himself; and what happy days those must have been ! It is hard to realize that time was when on this very spot there were birds by the thousands, and now often half a day goes by and not even one poor sparrow to make glad the fields. Many birds passed away with the trees, but not all. Birds have wit enough to accommodate themselves to very changed conditions, and would do so, but man will not permit. Very excellent evidence that mankind is not capable of taking care of itself, but needs an iron hand to keep it under control. We are continually prating about the blessings of liberty, but when do we ever hear of the curses of it ? Liberty has its well-defined boundaries, but these are ignored, and license and liberty are held as synonymous. Now, when it is almost, if not quite too late, an earnest cry is going up to spare the birds ; but are not the fools too many and the wise too few to restore our one-time blessing ? Spare what are left by all means, but what of those that are gone forever?

We establish national parks for the preservation of " noble game" when it is threatened with extinction, but had not wit enough to foresee the danger and check the lawless scoundrels who caused the mischief. Awake to the disappearing bison, because " noble game," but what of the nobility of singing birds? Is it never to be recognized? We do not seem to awake to this until the music ceases, and it dawns upon us that something is lacking to round out the summer day. A stranger from another planet might think that the " country" belonged to the city, and farmers were living in the fields by sufferance. Some heartless city clique demands bluebirds for bonnets, orioles for hats, and breasts of grebes for tippets, and these birds must yield their lives to meet such whims. He who loves the living bird is a fool and must stand aside. A celebration of some sort in Baltimore nearly caused the extermination of the Baltimore oriole.   Better exterminate——   But I forbear.

I can no longer see the milestone as it was. It forever brings to mind the one-time natural world, with all its beauties ; a thrilling thought while it stays, but ever followed by the sobering realization of naked and almost barren fields. Gaze intently at the milestone, and it will be replaced by the primitive forest and all wild life in its glory ; turn aside for an instant, break the spell, and what a dreary outlook is before us ! My milestone, about which I hoped to weave many a cheerful story, and with which I hoped to spend many a retrospective hour, is in very truth but a tombstone, recording how much has been lost to us, gone from us forever.

Christmas Out of Doors.

THAT bird is a bit of a philosopher that can stretch out its Christmas to three full months, and have the memory of it gladden all the rest of the year; that can get in its holiday a full month before we do ours, and keep it up for a good two months after our one little day. We have such a bird, a wren, cousin to the little chap that used to build in boxes, even in city yards.

Cheerfully, cheerfully, cheerfully! Hear its Christmas salutation, and who thinks of the dismal weather, even if snow be fathoms deep? *See to it, see to it, see to it!* Who can resist attending to such a command and keeping a merry countenance, even if there is no turkey for dinner? That wren's music will soften the hardest crust, and change what is very like a fast to a feast.

No holly or mistletoe, but why feel slighted? Here is black alder with as bright a berry, the whole bush like a ruddy flame that warms and lights the woodside glen, and here is moss as green as any sunny grass-plot of a May morning ; here, too, is Prince's pine and pipsissewa, and not a brown leaf in the woodland path but covers some fresh and frost-defying growth. Even in the open fields, tempest-swept and bleak under a cloudy sky, there is modest mullein, velvety and bright, that looks up at you like a winsome girl wrapped in her winter furs. We start out on a Christmas walk, thinking we will have to hunt for cheer, and find rather that our search must be for the truly desolate ; that is, if we want to nourish our pessimism among the wrecks and ruins of the dead summer ; and at every turn in our path, it may be, we will be urged to go yet farther afield by this good genius of a winter's day, the wren, that will call, when you least expect it, *Look here, look here, look here !* This is not silly fancy, nor overstraining of a wild bird's note to make it suit our whim. The Carolina wren has found the secret of a sweet content and would share it with the world.

Do not ask where this strange bird finds a

home,—whether in open fields or wooded hillside, by the wide river's bush-grown banks, or hides in hollows thick with tangled briers. I do not wish to track his wrenship to his lair. He is not a bird to be hunted, but let him find you out. Reverse the order, and be pursued rather than the pursuer. Now, he comes from the twiggy tops of twisted trees, and then, as if earth opened, he comes from some dark cave beneath you ; but whatever the direction, whatever the manner, the message that he brings is ever the same, let him express it as he will,—*Cheery, cheery, cheery !* and even the old oaks look glad. Whether or not, I feel so when I hear this earnest herald of a winter-long Christmas. Not all the sacred music of this day is to be heard in the churches. There is a real or supposed magic in green, and never a day in winter but we greet it effusively, as an ever welcome but unexpected gift. Are we logical ? We act as though we would all have headaches if the world was red, or become bilious beyond endurance if the skies were yellow, forgetting that the Eskimo finds a white world endurable ; so why not we, who hold ourselves so far in advance of hyperboreans, find the at present all prevailing browns of winter an inspiring color? It is not for a moment to be considered with reference to what has been or will be, but as to what is. Here we are, confronting a brown world this Christmas morning,—brown grass, brown weeds, brown everything,—and yet only regretfully, and loath to take up each object as it is and live in the present moment. If we could walk with the Carolina wren continually present, chiding our faint-heartedness, perhaps our illogic would not be overpowering. Do not wait, however, for the bird to call out *Look up at me, look up at me!* but remember its cheerful assurances at the outset and live only in the present moment; never indulge in a backward glance even mentally, nor, worse than all, wonder if your neighbor's fields are less brown than your own. Here you are, and a downright fool not to make the best of it. Let the path before you be the subject of a brown study, but do not let any element of a sad and sickly retrospection enter therein. Why, when grass is dead, does it turn brown and yellow rather than pink and purple?   Let such a question come to mind; puzzle over it, and see more in winter than a mere cemetery of the summer.   Do this, and you will not be so surprised at the Carolina wren's sudden outburst of *Cheerfully, cheerfully, cheerfully!* because you are now so cheerful yourself.

I fancy the attractiveness of in-door festivities of a Christmas Day will always be enhanced, by way of the contrast, if we have a Christmas outing in the same twenty-four hours.   We can better keep our own holiday if we know something of how Nature is celebrating hers.   Better this than by taking a nap after dinner, as we are apt to do.   Doubtless Nature sleeps in the moon and not even dreams, if astronomers are not mistaken, but here on earth one can find activity enough even in late December, if we know how to go in search of it.   The Carolina wren is sufficient of himself to guide you into paths of pleasantness and of surprisingly active celebrations of upland and meadow merriment, but never for one instant think this bird is left alone to keep creation in good spirits.   There is the cardinal, that whistles not to keep his courage up, but to keep his too great good spirits properly down ; transmuting his surplus energy to music that other creatures may share his happiness. Who, I wonder, can think his walk barren of attraction that has been saluted by a chickadee? Probably this has happened, but it is well to lend a patient ear to every bird that flies. Birds are not people, remember, and are in some things their superiors. There are those in this world who have judged and spoken hastily to unassuming people and lost thereby that for which they have been laboring half their lives. With but very few exceptions—none, with some people—our chickadee is the dearest of all the hundreds of birds that crowd about our home, and there should be no lack of company nor ground for complaint ; no excuse for loneliness on the rambler's part if even but one of these birds greets him in the woods or by the wayside. Christmas jollity extends over the whole winter with the chickadee. We make much of it to-day, and at most pick the bones of yesterday's turkey to-morrow. Why Christmas at all, if it preaches no sermon we can remember? The spirit of the day in us, it seems to be also in all we see. Even the solemn little red owl in the hollow apple-tree looks to-day less wise and more natural and happy, his big eyes reflecting the glow of winterberry and cedar and the green of the fresh grass spread now over the pebbly bed of the rippling brook. Not literally so, perhaps, but seemingly, because, in a happier mood ourselves, our own vision is clearer. We leave dull care behind us, and Nature then always looks kindly on our better selves. She has no patience with despondency, which is twin to cowardice, but meets cheerfulness face to face. When the storm comes the Carolina wren raises its voice. Are our activities roused in proportion as the tempest rages?

The in-door world to-day has a stronger claim than usual upon us. The coveted outing must be cut short, but better a crowded furlong than an empty mile, and no man has yet seen all that a furlong has to show. Eager to return, yet reluctant to leave the merry field and wood, it is well, perhaps, that Christmas comes but once a year.

The Charm of the Inexact.

WHEN a child of two or three is asked if it will have a cake, it naturally answers "Yes," but the cake is withheld until there is added to the original reply " Thank you, ma'am ;" all of which may be very polite, but is an infliction that the child should be spared. It is not what is said, but how it is said, that determines the mental status of the speaker. A simple "yes" or "no," as the case may be, spoken in a proper tone and with a meaning look, is better a thousand times over than, in reply to a simple question, to have a small vocabulary impatiently flung at you. We have but to listen to an ordinary conversation between a half-dozen couples in a room, and with our eyes shut we can imagine a battle royal between Webster, Worcester, and the several new dictionaries. We use too many words ; the trouble begins in infancy, and while then it is mere tautology and meaningless, it unavoidably develops a love of inexact statement, as when a child is found perfunctorily adding "I thank you" when it doesn't, and saying "yes" for politeness' sake, or to escape punishment, when its wishes call for "no."

I remember well, when a little boy, being asked by my mother if I did not want to go with Mrs. Bluemonday and carry her bundle. My reply was, "I do not want to go, but I can." Here was an exact statement of the conditions ; but I was roundly scolded for being so outspoken. Result, from that day I hated Mrs. Bluemonday.

The man who mentions but the plain fact, or is mathematically or monosyllabically inclined and says "warm" and "cool," meaning just this, for "hot" and "cold," not meaning those conditions,—such a person, I say, is invariably but most unreasonably voted a bore. He cannot meet our extravagant demands, requiring, as we do, recklessness of statement to rouse us to even a semblance of attention. The brilliant man, as he is popularly called, is too often but a polysyllabic chatterer. Fatigue never checks

his loquacity, but it is muscular rather than intellectual vigor that stands him so well in need.
Why?   If we go back to the starting-point of
our intellectual careers, we find that the natural
disposition to observe literally a scriptural in-
junction and let "yea" and "nay" suffice is
corrected, and we are forced to tack on a deal
that means nothing usually and sometimes is a
positive falsehood.   In short, the child that
would be terse and truthful is required to be
verbose and incorrect.   The Psalmist said in
his haste, "All men are liars:" if living now,
he could and would say it with justified delib-
eration.

As words are merely signs of our ideas and
we come quickly to understanding them, however improperly used, there is no serious harm
done, it is claimed ; but this we deny.   Least
of the ills is that most commented upon, the
development of a curious condition, the demand
for strong statement, for the use of even many
adjectives when none are called for.   In short,
we become charmed, as in the myth of the serpent exerting its power over birds, by the mere
tools of speech.   For this reason our language

appeals to the eye more than to the ear. As written, it is much more artistic than as spoken. We listen to the reading of printed matter with pleasure and profit, but when is conversation akin to this? I trust others have been more fortunate. I have not met a dozen persons who knew thoroughly well how to talk and gave me the feeling of having been fortunate because I had met them. Conversation should be worth the effort of utterance; but how seldom the outcome warrants the wear and tear of the machinery!

There is a ludicrous aspect of this whole question, attached almost exclusively to the conversation of women, which is perhaps a natural outcome of their inborn disposition to recklessness of statement, particularly where some immediate, petty advantage is to be gained, and total lack of heed as to the ultimate consequence. It required some months of constant observation, much commingling with womankind at popular gatherings, and a deal of listening unobserved when in stores and places of amusement, to determine the curious fact, as asserted by these women, that not one of them was ever startled by some sudden occurrence, but always "frightened to death." Never a woman because of a delayed meal felt the condition of hunger but was "almost starved;" she is never cold, but "positively frozen;" and so to the end of the chapter. The frequency of a woman's nearness to death is so marked, in her conversation, that when the critical time comes we imagine she ought from familiarity with the sensation to shuffle off this mortal coil with inexpressible ease and grace. And perhaps it is from this claimed familiarity that she is able to hoodwink the king of terrors, for she lives to be a hundred much more frequently than falls to the lot of men. But most remarkable of all of woman's peculiarities is the frequency with which she is "just crazy." The most trivial incident completely unbalances her, and all day long she is "just crazy" to see, to hear, to say, to do ; and it must be admitted that a great deal which she does and says does smack of lunacy. Perhaps it is this lack of absolute sanity that makes them so charming. Certainly there is some cause for it other than exquisitely adjusted mentality. Let us be thankful for the inexactitude of her self-condemnation as to sanity. She is always "just crazy," but generally sane enough to meet the approval of mankind. Why men never use these extravagant expressions I do not know. Is it because of the ounce or two more brain or an added convolution to the wrinkled mass?

This potent spell, this charm of the inexact, cast over us in early life, is the fountain-head of the all-prevalent insincerity that marks more or less every individual's career ; and, ungallant as it may seem to make the statement, this brief dealing with plain facts necessitates that women are to be placed in the front rank in this regard. Not a new bonnet at Easter or new dress at a reception but calls forth the " How lovely !" and " Perfectly exquisite !" that ripple charmingly from rosy lips, but did not bubble up from the heart. Alas, the fair creatures when they reach home say to themselves or to their sisters of this same bonnet or dress, "Wasn't it horrid ?" And in the crowded street, when they meet their acquaintances every one for the moment is their dearest friend, and the sole pleasure of the morning had been to meet them : out of hearing, how frequently this dearest friend is stabbed in the back ! How very wonderful and incomprehensible is this charm of the inexact, and how very unnecessary !

It may be objected that too precise statement would prove like the old-time Quaker garb, so monotonous that it would be depressing, and gayety shut out from the world. This seems reasonable at first glance, but if we practise moderation of speech and correctness of assertion, even very mildly, it will be found not so funereal as imagined. Our thoughtless chatter may be likened to the glare of sunshine ; our sober conversation to the refreshing shade.

Here is another view of the subject, and by no means an unimportant one. The world at large would be less ignorant if fact and theory could forever be kept separate and apart until the latter has passed its probationary stages and been raised to the state of fact-hood. But they are not kept apart and radically distinct, they keep knowledge in a turmoil, and prove, sadly enough, that where ignorance is bliss, 'tis folly to be wise. Those who read our newspapers and periodical publications find it difficult to equip themselves with the facts of any case, seeing how fiercely disputed is every statement of a fact as such.   Those who have had experience in any line of research know the bewildering array of opinions daily set forth, and how persistently the theorists hound every one who ventures to question their hobbies by virtue of the obvious facts resulting from their own observations.   To defy the truth and defame the truthful that theory may remain ascendant and the fathers of theories hold to high places is one of the melancholy features of prevalent inexact statement.   This phase indeed calls for strong language, and it is unfortunate that it is not legally permissible.   A vast deal of the ignorance that is now prevalent is due to the impudence of those who have really no authority to express an opinion.   Barnum, it was, I believe, who said people liked to be humbugged; but did not this refer to matters of mere amusement,—tricks that we were always expecting to solve and so set ourselves aright? So far no harm is done, but not so when the truth is held back because here and there some opiniative " professor" must needs confess himself mistaken. This is everywhere a feature of inexact statement that is not charming, but disgusting, to those who finally discover for how long a time they have been duped by dishonest "authorities" on the subject.

The Rustic: a Protest.

BY mere accident my eye caught the definition of "Rustic" in Stormonth's Dictionary, and I, being a countryman, at once rebelled. "Rude, untaught, awkward, unadorned." Perhaps it was unwise, but at the time, and still, I feel warranted in talking back, and am moved to declare the definition, as it stands without any mollifying comment, undeserved. But my protest must have a beginning that is respectful, if emphatic, and to maintain with proper dignity the rustic's point of view I will start with the assertion that the dictionary's statement, standing without qualification, is not true. If the rustic is all that is here said of him, it means, as compared with city folk, and what a difference that makes! Why cannot I, a rustic, look depreciatingly at the folks in town? As a matter of fact, I have never done anything else.

The rustic is not necessarily rude. He may

be plain-spoken, but not offensively so. He may look you straight in the eye, but he does not impudently stare, and there is herein a wonderful difference not always recognized within city limits. Honest himself, he expects honesty in you, and, speaking the truth, neither blushes in so doing nor expects that his words will cause you to be confused. If this is rudeness, let us have more of it.

Untaught ! True, he may never have heard of Homer, and is in doubt if Shakespeare is the author of dramas, or is a play of that name. Never mind. The rustic makes a remark at odd times that Shakespeare would have been delighted to have thought of. Shockingly untaught ! Yes ; but what is ancient literature to him who has been reared in the still older literature of a bird's song and the murmur of the breeze in the pine-tree tops that shade his cottage ? If untaught as to the past, in an historical sense, he is not ignorant of the present, and his arguments in times of political turmoil are worthy of attention. It seems not to occur to some people that the rustic has no special edition of the metropolitan dailies printed to meet the requirements of his supposed inferiority. And, to be less serious, how effectually he silences many a college-bred theorist who applies his knowledge of Nature to the rustic's farm.

"There ought to be clay near the surface here and rock cropping out over yonder, and your soil is better adapted to grass than grain," the rustic is informed.

"Ought to be, did you say, sir? Well, perhaps; only it ain't so. There's no clay nor rocks within sight, and I grow better wheat than hay."

The college man is not silenced. How could a rustic accomplish that? Perhaps he thinks the man is lying, and he continues, patronizingly, "Your brook is too small for anything but minnows, and all the game's killed off, of course."

"Good-sized minnies, sir, in that ditch in the pastur' meadow; big enough for pan fish, so the folks say, when I bring up a mess of pike, a pound a-piece or more ; but you're right about game. There's no deer nor bears, but when the season comes in, I look a bit after the quail and woodcock and rabbits and the like. Farm work's pretty much done up in October, and I don't mind takin' a day off."

How very rude, thinks the college man; but stay, where really was the rudeness? Does it not lie at the door of the townsman who comes to the country thinking that every rustic is a fool? There is not one word to be said against colleges and the education to be received there, but it must not be supposed that no portion of that same lore can be gathered without the aid of a text-book. Given a desire for knowledge and it can be had by any one at head-quarters, from Mother Earth herself, as well as from class-rooms where it is filtered through a professor's brain.

An untaught rustic is but another name for an idiot, and unless in charge of a caretaker would soon die of starvation. The knowledge derived by close contact with Nature may not fit us for the extremes of artificiality of the city; may leave the ear untrained for the opera but not unappreciative of the Thrush; may knot the knuckles, to the destruction of kid gloves, but harden them to effectiveness when brought face to face with danger. The rustic's eye may not follow the cunning of the landscape spread upon canvas, but it notes the changing scene as the seasons pass, and makes the rustic the reliable guide if you would know where the sweetest fruits and brightest flowers are found; and it is not an unknown occurrence for the museum-lounging naturalist to experience a set-back when he airs his science in the rustic's hearing. Untaught, yes; we admit it, but every inch a man. Do those from the city always bear measuring by the same standard? Is the rest from toil less wholesome, more animal-like, less worthy of a man, sought in the rude rocker of hickory splints, than that, too often sought in vain, on velvet cushions? It is a matter of difference of education, of tastes in opposite directions, but is there less manliness? Is the rustic really lower in the scale? Is being nearer to Nature lower than being part and parcel of a town? The most fastidious can pass weeks with a rustic and yet never have a fair opportunity to criticise adversely one word or deed. That the " untaught" condition of the rustic, as viewed by the city man, signifies lack of refinement and necessitates it, is positively untrue.   He may be plainer spoken, may never attempt to chase the devil around the stump, but his words are no more offensive than the vagueness of the town-dweller's redundant phrases.   If they are offensive, then the hearer is more open to criticism than the speaker.   Unto the honest all things are honest, and the defect lies with those whose thoughts are led into miry paths because of honest speech uttered with no trace or thought of extended construction.   No ; the "untaught" rustic has a good deal to be thankful for, having honesty sufficient to look the world squarely in the eye and speak plainly.   It is an inestimable privilege, and he who takes offence is a fool.

The author of my dictionary is not content with calling the rustic he had in mind rude and untaught, but he is awkward !   Whether this is a greater or less defect than the others I do not know, but it stands equally prominent upon the printed page.   Awkward !   I admit he might not pass through a crowded parlor without jostling the elbow of some slender fop of the city, or worse, might tread upon that abomination of fashion, a lady's train ; he might, but only with grave misgiving, be trusted to pass a cup of coffee through a surging crowd of hungry mortals. It were better not to trust him. Yes; awkward when he feels out of place, and who is not? But I have seen this awkward rustic pick up a light rifle—rifle, mind; not shot-gun— and bring down a teal that was flying at the rate of a mile a minute; have seen him drive his team afield and plough a furrow, without other guide than his eye, as straight as the best surveyor could have staked it out. I have seen him cut a slender switch, and with a fuzzy string from the grocer's counter make tackle that wound deftly in and out among the overhanging tangle of brush, and bring to his creel the trout that had teased and tormented the skilled angler. Awkward, yes; where the artificialities of town are concerned, but scarcely so when near to Nature. There he treads the earth with that confidence in his strength which makes him bold as a lion where bravery is called for, and gentle as a lamb to all the unoffending world.

Not content with the triple charge, that, if true, would be too great a load to carry, the author of the dictionary adds that the rustic is unadorned.   We know all too well there is truth in this charge.   There is no ring on his finger, no diamond on his shirt front; the cuffs are buttoned, or there may be no cuffs at all; there are no tanned shoes polished with lemon juice or banana peel; no golf stockings or cycling suit; not a trace of evidence that Fashion has been ever heard of; but there is a glitter in the eye that outsparkles the diamond; there is the line of strength in every muscle if not the line of beauty, and through the sunburn that has reddened his face shines an honest purpose that fills his whole life; an adornment that is too often lacking when we pass the boundary that divides town and country.   It may be true, but is it pity that the rustic is rude, untaught, awkward, and unadorned, when, with all these blemishes, he knows no fear, and in time passes to another world without thought of cringing, but to look directly in the face, all unabashed, whomsoever he may meet in the realms of eternity?

How true it is that the rustic loses when he goes to town ! with the man of the city it is all gain when he goes into the country.   Lay prejudice aside. Be honest for the moment, if not too great an effort, and see if the rustic, as painted in the dictionary, loses so very much when compared with the finished product of metropolitan humanity.

The Unlettered Learned.

CRUDITY of diction is not always indicative of crudity of thought. The latter has been longer in the world than language, for the prime·val savage was not without the elements of mind when gestures and grunts were his sole means of expression. To rebel is as human as to err, and he who defies grammar is not neces·sarily a fool. How often we hear it said, " Oh, he's an uneducated man," and so pay no serious attention to what this " unfortunate" may have to say. It may happen that we suffer more than he does by such assumed superiority. The round of the seasons can effect as much as a college curriculum to an open-eyed man. Not in the same direction, not with equal artistic finish, but fool himself who sets down the un-tutored student of the out-door world as little better than a fool. By syntax and prosody we cannot solve the problem of an oak-tree, or

226

that of the minnow in the brook that flows past its gnarly roots. Greek philosophy does not explain the color of a flower, nor Roman sophistry why birds build nests.

Granted the desirability of all the intellectual culture that centres in a university library, still it is not indispensable when we take to the woods and have a desire to know more of the planet on which we live ; for this self-same earth was a very complete affair and well worthy of a place in the universe when the anthropoid ape was the climax of evolutionary activity. Had man never been, no reasoning creature from Mars, we will say, could have thought of the incompleteness of earth or supposed it was yet to be the scene of higher intellectual activities ; or, if the world had come to an end in the days of continued struggle with wild beasts, of cavedwelling and cannibalism, it could not have been said of the planet that it had closed its career untimely ; nor, later, in the dawn of education, could this have been said. Some nineteen hundred years ago the end of the world was confidently expected by a few thousands of world-weary enthusiasts.

Before the day of schools and colleges there were unlearned men who knew a vast deal, after their own fashion ; and this is equally true of to-day.   The world has waited for wireless telegraphy and the electric motor, but it did not need to.   The north pole is no longer a mystery, but many have lived who were ignorant of all this, yet spoke words of wisdom.   The ice of the mill-pond whispers the essentials of a frozen ocean.   Many have walked boldly to a fact and by unschooled cunning captured it. Now, the bicycle carries us across the continent, but the only gathered fact is that we are transported.   Eyes and ears are no longer the open avenues to the brain.   Life is more a matter now of heels than of head.

The man who has spent a long life in the country, with his fields bounded by woodland and swamp, though he can neither read nor write, is not necessarily ignorant.   Nature has made so much of her working plain to his untutored mind that he can interpret in a way of his own, and a way, too, that is not bewildering by reason of a long array of contradictory statements.   It is something to have knowledge all your own, gathered wholly by your unaided efforts : it makes one free ; for he who merely echoes another's thoughts, or accepts the dictum of another as to what is true and what is false, is in a sense a slave. The authorities, as they assert themselves to be, are ever tyrants ; our manhood is in proportion to our independence of any and all arbiters. The submissive man is a mere machine. To shape our lives at the direction of others that we may be wise and saved, is to keep ourselves ignorant and unworthy of salvation. Knowledge direct from Nature is a source of satisfaction as unfailing as a great library is to a student of books. When the uneducated man who lives in the open country lays by his work for the day, he can turn to himself for amusement, and often with satisfaction equal to his who turns to the printed thoughts of other people.

I do not undervalue what the world calls "education." Lacking it myself, I may be calling down condemnation upon my head for speaking of it as I do. I never had a teacher who gave me the slightest encouragement, and more than one was a brute in human form. I know nothing of college life beyond vague hearsay; but, although it seemed to be expected, I never trembled in the courts of classic greatness. It is no part of evolution that all men should be of one pattern. There are oak-trees and people who live in their company, and smaller folk who linger in the shade of shrubbery; there are toilers in the field as well as in the town, and the place of each is equally well defined. Homer, in the library, for him who loves Homer; but the thrush's song, in the tangle of green brier, is sufficient for my needs. I may be less a man, but is this being less not a part of the scheme of the world? I do not feel my littleness. But I would speak of others, not of myself.

Lack of guidance derived from books is not a synonyme of mental inferiority or degradation, as some would put it. The "ignoramus" who cannot speak correctly can send the bullet of his thought straight home, if he does use as a means of so doing an obsolete flint-lock musket instead of the improved Winchester rifle. We pay too little attention to the fact that a man's purpose is accomplished, and criticise too much the manner of its bringing about. Words are signs of ideas : the crude speech that makes me wiser is more welcome than the polished phrase that tells me nothing but what I knew before, or leaves me in doubt whether it is sense and sound, or sound that lacks sense.

" But," speaks up some one learned in book-lore, " without an arbiter there must be con-fusion, an inextricable confusion of fact and fancy."

" Thanks for the suggestion," I reply, "but by what authority does your arbiter dare to deter-mine which is true and which is false?" Really, if we ponder reverently, patiently, and of our own accord, unmoved by others' urgency, over the tomes of Solons dead and gone, shall we find harmony? The sages of the past are called authorities. Over what? By what authority are they so called? Not by common consent. That never yet has been accorded to any man. Not a fact was ever set before the world but it gave rise to at least two opinions, and usually to ten times as many more. Truth is a plant of slow growth, and man's gardening improves neither its stalk nor its blossom. No one can change to sweetness the bitterness of its fruit, or, on the other hand, embitter its sweetness. The unassuming man of the backwoods, whom we hold as ignorant, may not be able to separate paste from diamonds, but both are sources of genuine pleasure, and an arbiter, even if such a character had or could have other than earthly authority, would only take away the paste and lessen by a large fraction the delight or satisfaction in life of the so-called ignorant man.

But why forever drawing the distinction between the ignorant and the learned, between wisdom and foolishness, the true and the untrue? Do not the mightiest in the world of scholars hug delusions? It is ever a matter of almost all-wise but never quite so. We say of many, "If"—and nothing further is necessary. If, then, greatness hugs delusion, why may not littleness cling to the self-taught "ignoramus" of the woods and fields? The unlettered learned has his place in the world; the untutored aristocrat does not lack in wholesome dignity. Ignorance has proved the guide to truth too often to be spurned as useless. I have met with many unschooled men, talked with them, listened to them, and the world was fuller of meaning to me because of them.   They are still so vividly impressed upon my memory that when wisdom makes the world unlovely (no uncommon occurrence) I turn to those whose ignorance has proved a blessing to them, and so full a one that in no stinted measure they share their joy with me.

Uz Gaunt, the Humboldt of his township, Miles Overfield, the Cuvier of Crosswicks Creek, were the truly great men of my boyhood's days, greater by far, to me, than the "intellectual giants" I have met since then.   I say this with all due respect for those now living, for these men of my days of hero-worship told me what I wished to know, and what they told me became then and there gospel that I have not since learned to look upon askance because of the higher criticism natural to maturer years. And then, alas ! to-day's Solons are all at loggerheads about such things as have ever interested me the most.   I greet with hearty laughter now the thought that the simple explanations of that unlettered yet really learned Uz Gaunt stand the test of time and of hostile criticism.

Miles Overfield knew every tree on the broad reach of meadows, and what each one was to every bird and beast of the wide waste of swamp and weedy pasture. There was not a bird that nested here but he could lead me to its haunts, nor mink or muskrat, opossum, skunk, or raccoon, but he knew where it hid by day and where by night it was likely to wander. A hunter, in all this, but this was not all. He discerned their relations to one another and to the world at large. No mere hunter, bent only upon his game with all the savagery of hawks bent upon their prey, but a naturalist in the widest sense, taking comprehensive views of what lay before him; grasping with quick intelligence a fact, and—what mankind so generally fail to do—grasping its full significance, the relation of one fact to all others. Since his primer was tossed aside with a shout of joy, as of a prisoner set free, his eyes had seldom rested on a printed page, and never quite understandingly; yet Miles Overfield, though unlettered, was not unlearned. A congregation of scientists might have confused him, could they have cornered him in their book-lined halls; but what of these

men singly, did they meet him in the open field?
There would not come one specialist but he
could lead him to spots that would delight the
student's heart and open up to him new views
of their common treasure-house, the out-door
world.

By both Gaunt and Overfield technical details
were overlooked, perhaps their existence was
never suspected; the scholars' fine philosophy
never entered their dreams. That far, they were
abundantly happy in their ignorance. As to
the great mystery that encompasses the whole
earth and the heavens above the earth, they
were wisely content to leave to eternity to
make clear whatsoever time withheld from
them. These men realized their limitations,
and did not presume to lead me beyond facts
about which there could be no discussions;
facts that met every requirement of my life
then; facts that were sources of joy then, and
must remain to me as such until I have joined
my unlettered friends; and I ask no better company, if company we have, in the land of the
hereafter.

The Comfort of Old Clothes.

HOW far do we think our own thoughts; how far repeat to ourselves the thoughts of others, thinking we are dealing with original impressions? Is there anything new under the sun? It is an open question, but there are some things remaining among us that are old—as one's old clothes. For one I am thankful—not an ever-present sensation—for my share; but we all have them, inasmuch as not until garments are old do we lay them aside. When they are worn out, in my neighbors' estimation, I begin to love clothes dearly. Not until every trace of newness is gone are they an essential part of me; in other words, do we become acquainted and work in perfect harmony. We are righteously indignant when unreasonably restrained; patience at such a time being but admission that we are weaklings and require a guardian. I, for one, have no time to spend in bending the tailor's lack of skill to the shape of my shoulders, and new clothes are valueless, an infliction, metal yet in the ore, until they become old, and then their value is inestimable. Rebel as I will against having aught to do with it, I have at intervals to conquer this obnoxious newness, and perhaps I am fairly well repaid; but then comes the hour of my trial.   When I have come off conqueror and more than conqueror, I am told that I need a new suit; or, in plain English, the recent torture is to be repeated.   But I am not conquered.   I am rich now in that I have two old coats, and there shall be no divorcement.   Until death do us part, as young people promise, so I promise myself. The world may go hang, but I will be happy as a king.   My coat knows me and I know my coat.   It is not mere toleration on either part, but mutual good-will and respect.   It is a whim of mine to believe my old coats are happy because they fit, and I am happy that they are an aid and not a hinderance.   A man is known by the company he keeps, so let me be known by my close association with old clothes.   If you that worship immaculate cloth and glory in the newness thereof chance to see me coming, walk on the other side of the road. Do not seek, but shun me. I am too happy to be disturbed.

Do not talk to me about coats fitting as neatly to the body as the bark of a beech-tree to the trunk thereof. My skin does that, and what I ask for in a coat is the loose and careless hang of the lichens that find lodgement on the beech's bark, or the moss that rests lightly at the roots of the tree. There is a fine old sassafras that stands before me whenever, at home, I turn eastward, going out of doors. From top to toe it is draped with a creeping vine that hangs in graceful folds; the tree a noble Roman, with an artistic toga. That tree tells me daily how desirable is flexibility in clothing, and yet I am urged—and sometimes submit—to an unyielding collar that tortures my neck, and box in my wrists as if every bone was broken and needed artificial support. It is bad enough to be really injured and have to be boxed up and braced until the bones are knitted and strong again, but to imitate all this and to be be-collared, be-cuffed, and be-bosomed by a laundryman and then smile and be happy is really beyond my power.   I do not criticise my neighbors, but I do ask and insist for myself flexibility of covering, and indulge in no end of honest, outspoken profanity when I cannot have it. We do not value our independence sufficiently. The world is not yet powerful enough to down genuine talent. To a certain extent every man can be a law unto himself and yet not a failure in the race of- life. His clothing can come within the limit. Let him wear his coat honestly. Let his proper self shine through that coat to the pleasure and profit of his friends, and the antique cut of the garment will not be an eyesore unto them. If it is, then your coat more than yourself is valued, and your friends can be dispensed with without serious loss to yourself. He who is rebelliously disposed and possesses an inquiring mind will be astonished at the reception such views will meet with from his fellow-freemen. Free? However smooth the current, let but the tiniest twig fall upon it and its surface is ruffled ; so the bare mention of a counter-current thought disturbs at once the placid serenity of our spiritless compliance to whatsoever has been laid down as law. Once, when I spoke of the comfort of old clothes, not a friend but frowned, looking anxiously at his broadcloth, and daintily tweaked the spear-points of his faultless collar.

Old clothes, not out-worn or threadbare or offensively soiled, but old in the sense of adapted or ripened, so that your coat is conformable, an extra-cuticular garment that is twin to your skin and not a veneer merely that is cross-grained and rebellious, contesting every extension and expansion of the wrinkles Nature has given the only covering she allows you on your entrance into this vale of sorrows. We take time to do everything that we must do, to live ; and why not allow time for your coat to settle to a realization of what is expected of it? Occasionally a mania for that which is old takes strong possession of a community, and many a mortal wishes first and then swears that he does belong to an old family; so why not extend this merit of age to more of life's minor considerations than we do. We prattle in a childish way about old friends and old associations, as if necessity was a common feature of mankind ; so why not some other matters. Grandfather's clock tells the hours more musically than does a cheap Yankee rattle-trap that ticks in a way suggestive of Walt Whitman's barbaric yawp,— so, I say, why so impatient when old clothes are mentioned?   Scott, in the "Surgeon's Daughter," makes a character in the story remark, "Old recollections are like old clothes and should be sent off wholesale."   I do not believe it.   The future is unknowable, we live only in the present, but we have come out of the past, and so long as I keep dragging myself out of this past I purpose pulling my old coat with me, nor ask when I shall let go my hold and renew the vexations incident to the putting on of a new garment.

Not long since I was poking about in the mud, tracing the course of a mole that had burrowed and uplifted the earth directly after a prolonged midwinter rain, when I was imperiously hailed by a stranger and asked who lived at the end of the lane, pointing with his carriage whip directly towards my house.   I meekly replied "I do," and watched the movements of a black-hawk that was sailing past.

"I don't mean the tenant house," the stranger replied, impatiently.

"There is none on the place," I remarked, poking into a hole in the ground, where possibly lurked a meadow-mouse.

"This is where Dr. Abbott lives, is it not?" the stranger then asked in a more natural tone, for I saw he had been putting on airs.

"It is," I replied.

"Do you know if he is home?" he asked.

"I know that he is not," was my answer.

The stranger looked much disappointed; and as he had evidently hired a horse at the livery and was not some nearby chatterbox, I felt moved to tell him all the truth, and so, after a pause, added, "I am the man you wish to see."

His "Oh !" still rings in my ears.

We had a pleasant afternoon, and I learned more from him than he gathered from my words, and I do not feel mortified to have been found in a mud-bespattered coat. It is astonishing how constantly some people are "mortified," but I have noted that the process never goes even skin deep, for now these many years, it is not yet to be detected beyond mere words, which I hold as lightly as I value the comfort of old clothes.

In deep, dark woods.

In Deep, Dark Woods.

FEW men and a forest; many men and a desert. So it seems, to the regret of those who have a greater liking for Nature than for artificiality; for the earth with Nature as a caretaker rather than endless fields under man's supervision. Woods both deep and dark are not of necessity a matter of long ago, known to us but by hearsay, nor need they be boundless in extent or the growth of centuries. Nature can readily rebuild when man relinquishes his hold, and though the farmer has drained the last drop of life-blood from the long-suffering soil, Nature knows where the overlooked springs of fertility lie hidden, and, seeking their aid, by her chemic art distils vigor from earth and air that defy man's efforts. Let him withdraw, and, on the barren soil amid the few foul weeds that stand, suggestive grave-marks to departed worth, anew will spring up the pine and beach and oak. I have seen a flourishing mulberry that had forced its way through a neglected pavement. A deep dark woods may be a new forest; clustered trees, not older than the rambler that lingers in their shade, yet literally dark and deep, for a narrow strip of woodland may be both if you stand at one end and only look towards the other. We need a little tact when giving a loose rein to the imagination. As children say, we must "make believe," and by so doing a dozen acres are as suggestive as that many square miles. We must concern ourselves with what is near at hand and distinctly in view, not bother about the boundaries ; study the hub and spokes of the wheel, and not wonder about the mud on the tire.

It may be well to realize, before you enter, that here, as in the open, you are not a lord of creation, but one of many in a mixed crowd, and not a very important one at that. No tree steps aside at your approach nor moves a limb from your path if it happens to obstruct it. You must pick and push your way through, and if a bended branch can fly back and strike you, it will do so and stands unmoved however

fiercely you may frown.   It lessens the conceit
that mars every man to walk in the woods.
The fact that these trees are here by right and
you are an intruder is very forcibly set before
you.   Nevertheless a forest is not inhospitable.
A dead tree may fall and crush you, but that
was because you were not forelearned in wood-
lore.   If killed or maimed, it was not through
malice aforethought.   Satisfaction, in this world,
is too rare to miss any opportunity to acquire
even a trace of it, so take what you can from
the gruesome thought that a dead branch of a
tree may fall on you, but the result is purely
accidental.   There is really something in the
thought, if it cannot mend a broken head.

On the excellent principle of "contented wi'
little and cantie wi' mair," I have been wandering in the woods, and here, let me say, even a
single tree means a vast deal on a hot, sunny
summer day.   The difference in temperature
from sunshine to shade is often startling.
Under some lone amid-field oak the coolness
of October lingers, though it is tropical beyond
the tree's shadow.   What a tree means is not
to be realized in a moment, so, how hopeless,

even in a lifetime, to attempt to solve the problems of a forest ! It is far more satisfactory to study ten oaks for ten years than gallop on horseback through a grove of ten thousand. If you must satisfy the modern mania for numbers, take to counting the leaves. It needs but a few trees to give you one million or more. What has just been said of content is something more than a catchy phrase.

There are other than laboratory methods of studying Nature, and he is lacking who can sit at the foot of an old tree and get no hints of what the tree signifies as part of the world's stupendous whole. It is something more than fuel or lumber, for it is the living tree with which he is or ought to be dealing. How very different, as a specimen impression, one of a hundred, are the trunks of our deciduous forests! It is only the oaks that offer me a comfortable resting-place on their roots. They offer both seats and backs of a very easy chair, but the beeches and birches, backs only. The curiously twisted roots, with deeply grooved bark, like models of the Colorado cañon, extend in many directions from the oaks of my home hill-side, and might readily be classified as the furniture dealer does the chairs, sofas, and couches of his stock in trade. I have them all here, and if not elaborately upholstered, they are at least strongly put together, equal to all reasonable demands upon them, and can we say this of all the joiner-work that finds place in houses? No oak-root chairs have ever creaked because I sat down too suddenly, but if they did there would follow no black looks from the hostess because of my lack of care. To sit in the woods, then, and on a safe and sound seat, has this additional merit, we do not sit in silence, even if we so elect. If no living creature comes to at least so much as look at you, your own thoughts will keep you company. The wind that gently stirs the branches of a forest will make you think, however assiduously you may court dreamless sleep, and thoughts born in such a place, at such a time, are never unworthy of your better self. Is it true that you cannot, however hard you try, think when alone in deep, dark woods? Be careful how you admit it, lest it be wondered if you ever think at all.

So suggestive is every woodland tract that

the approach thereto is not to be overlooked because we are bent upon penetrating its recesses. Against the dark background of my present outlook, formed by the rim of a small but ancient wood, I see the restless herons that look black as crows, passing from their nesting trees in an upland sink-hole to the meadows. They make so pretty a picture that I forget the background for a time, and am reminded of it when a wary crow dashes impetuously by or darts from sight through some slight opening in the leafy wall, or a woodland bird seeks the upper air and then sinks into the green depths beneath it. As usual, when out of doors I am indebted to some bird for what I most value of out-door knowledge, and I remember that before me, though hidden as yet, is a winding roadway, gloomy and long neglected, but a roadway still, though those who habitually used it have been dead for a century. While yet afield, I always notice with more than idle curiosity any long forest wall. Somewhat strangely, it does not give the impression of an obstruction to progress in that direction, as does your neighbor's fence with "keep off" dotted over it.

The woods you come to, seen from the open fields, is not a mere barrier to further fieldward progress, but the beginning of a new order of things, and, much as I love the open fields, I am moved to say, a better order. It is with a sense of relief I enter a woodland tract. The trace of the primeval savage, still lingering in human nature, comes to the surface when we breathe the woodsy air with its subtle distillation of undiscoverable sweets, and then leaving the mossy ground, and taking a seat on some extended limb, what endless fancies in the brief hour of an arboreal existence! The passion for tree-climbing so pronounced in youth is a serious loss when discarded in our maturer years. The whole face of the country changes at fifty feet from the ground, but who at fifty ventures to climb a tree? More's the pity, for pleasures are not too many that even one can be spared.

Occasionally an exploratory impulse takes hold of me and I lose myself in a wilderness of tangled underbrush, having only so much sky above me as the interlacing of tree-tops permits. Nor is this child's play. We have but to consider for a moment the depth, height, and width of our ignorance even of the garden's gooseberry hedge to effectually cure us of walking with the air of a philosopher in the deep, dark woods. When an oak has whispered all the secrets of the plant world we can hope to ramble understandingly in field or forest, and not before.

Having entered the woods, the new atmosphere revives the sluggish senses that have wearied of sunny fields. Appreciation of details takes the place of vague generalization. At this point stands a sentinel tulip-tree, a landmark for miles around it. No human structure commands such instant attention. A procession winding among cathedral pillars is but a tawdry imitation of the vine clinging to its towering trunk, and wheezy music from a loft a sorry echo of the morning breeze. Yet how meagre a congregation has even an aged tree, even one that has sheltered the homestead for generations. Rarely do we see two or three even gathered to consider it, and when such gathering occurs it is not always fit audience though few. When Philander Pointblank, a quaint character of

years ago, persisted in sitting in the shade of
the old oak in the meeting-house yard, while
the Friends were gathered in the building, he
was not so illogical as his people thought him.
He maintained that the shade of a living oak
was as fit a spot wherein to worship as "a pen
made of the carcasses of a hundred dead ones."
Philander was long a concern upon the minds
of his co-religionists, and it is rather noteworthy
that he alone of his contemporaries is remembered.   Not like so many, too near to nothing
to be friends or foes.   Extremely ignorant, men
call him ; but I hold him as a real philosopher.
Not because of his fancy for the old oak, but
because of that infatuation which will not admit
that in all things art is an improvement over
Nature.   Philander Pointblank knew both inti-
mately and remained loyal to the out-door
world.   The tears that he shed when the lightning destroyed the favorite oak of his little
woodland tract were more honest than many
his neighbors have shed at funerals.   When I
said as much in my address at Philander's
funeral, there was a great raising of eyebrows
and some shuffling of feet, but no one was

candid enough to admit the truth of my assertion ; strong negative evidence that what I said
was true.

Beyond the entrance to this ancient wood,
where grass gives way to patches of gray moss,
to sphagnum ; where the water lies in pools,
and lichens so wrinkled and dead white they
suggest fragments of cast-off skin rather than a
living growth ; underbrush, shrubs of a dozen
species, and a bewildering array of tree-trunks.
The latter are as individual as men upon a
crowded street.   It is more difficult to find two
alike than to note a marked resemblance among
people.   Then, never to be overlooked, in every
sense, is the leafy canopy, effectual against the
direct rays of the sun to such degree that a dim
but not obscuring light prevails ; one that opens
your eyes and leads to quicker perception of
the objects crowded about you.   Less escapes
one's notice now than in the glaring sunshine
of the open fields.   The white of many a woodland blossom fairly glows, and every purple or
rosy bloom likewise glows with a warmth not
common to the flowers of the meadow or the
roadside.   Dogwood, in May, when the foliage

is fully grown, fairly glitters with stars that may be seen half a mile away. The pink azalea, when seen against a background of dark mosses, stands out so boldly that not the deepest shadows of densest forest growth obscures their outline, and what jolly sport to trace a grape-vine from its anchorage to the airy terminations in some distant tree-top! It is not well to give the measurements that I have recorded in note-books. Let him who is curious solve the problem of a grape-vine's whereabouts when lost among the branches of old trees, and determine, too, the length of the vine as it twists and turns and returns, and shoots upward again. This following of a long serpent-like growth leads to curious places and unsuspected conditions, and the truth is brought to us that trees are something more than trunk and branches. If it is in early summer, the chances are that you will be led to some cunningly concealed nest of a vireo, and it was while tracing a grape-vine that I found my first nest of a blue-gray gnatcatcher—a rare find here—high up in a tulip-tree. Before I saw the nest I had neither seen nor heard the birds, although passing near by, for weeks, almost every day ; and, of course, this is likely to prove true of other vines, a fact all too apt to be overlooked. The poison-ivy climbs to the very top of many a large tree and in time appears to smother it. This growth, like a huge hairy serpent, clings so tenaciously to some oaks I have seen that all my strength was necessary to detach it. It certainly appears, in time, to kill the tree it encircles, but I am not positive ; but this is not true of the Virginia creeper. Near my home is a sassafras, just seventy feet high, and for twenty years the creeper has mingled its leaves with those of the tree's outermost and uppermost twigs. When the autumnal coloring occurs, there is a mingling of dark red and yellow that is worth a day's journey to see.

The dim light of deep, dark woods has been much written about, but it is dimness that does not obscure. I have found it a developing light that brings the minor details into satisfactory prominence. If color is important in determining the identity of an object, we can be sure in the woods, when it would be a matter of doubt in the open fields. This is peculiarly true of the birds about us. I have seen many a cardinal, tanager, and rose-breasted grosbeak that looked black as night in the open fields, but there is no mistaking their colors when flitting across our path here in the woods. Let a cardinal red-bird perch on a low branch, in full view, and red he will appear, as he proves to your delighted ear his claim to past master in the art of whistling. The brown and white of the melancholy thrush, even of the little tree-creeper, can be traced feather by feather, and the passing warblers, spotted and streaked like the harlequins, show themselves in their true colors when in the woods. There is no glare of the sun's direct light to bewilder you, to blind you for the moment, when you could best have seen the restless bird. So accurately adjusted are your senses to their surroundings that life and the world take on a new meaning. The song of a bird is so delightful that it might seem at first thought that the conditions under which it is heard were quite immaterial. Sitting on a porch, in an easy-chair, with the purple light of the dying day making fairy-land alike of all the outlook, the matchless strains of the thrush's evening song heard upon the upland lawn may seem the climax of kind Nature's melody; but wander at this time to the nearest woodland tract; rest by the trunks of majestic time-honored beeches, known as "the Three Beeches" so long ago as 1689, where the shade at noontide is scarcely less sombre than the shadows of night, and hear this same song of the evening thrush, or listen to the rosebreast as he breathes his love strain to his hidden mate; yes, hear even the' forest peewee or the dream song of a sparrow, and there will be revealed to you what magic, that spurs to full activity our every sense, lies in the dim but searching light of deep, dark woods.

I suppose the woods in winter figure more in literature than in the actual experiences of readers. These same woods are just as deep, but not so dark, during the pleasant days of January, and particularly after a deep snow. The arctic conditions are now all underfoot or immediately about us, and a thoroughly cheerful, if not exactly summery, condition overhead. Certainly there is no suggestion of gloom Tartarian which few can rid of hobgoblins; this is

Woods during pleasant January days.

a matter more natural to leafy June, absurd as it really is, but now, even if forced to wallow in deep snow that blots out the familiar beaten

path, still your reward is certain. The woods in winter! There is a ring in the very words that is exhilarating. The individuality of every tree is now pronounced. The smooth, wrinkled, dark and light barks are distinct, and each asks for consideration based on its own merits, and not as an humble factor in the production of a general effect. The lichened, mottled gray of oaks suggesting comfort rather than conformity to fashion; the tight-fitting uniform of the stately beech; the ragged yellow birch that flaunts its tatters as if proud to wear them; here, surely, are variety and proud independence worthy of your attention. Here, now, are these trees as we see gatherings of men. They are not bare in the sense of nakedness; the leaves are gone, but this is simply the doffing of hat and cloak. In winter, in the woods, with snow a foot deep, I can talk to a tree as I would to my neighbor, meeting him at his ease, in-doors. It may seem a childish whim to talk to trees; literally, it is; but trees can tell us a great deal if we will only stop by them for a moment. This hollow oak has a nest of squirrels twenty feet above me, a fact worth knowing, and the tree has this same fact written out upon its trunk. The snow is scattered about, but not by wind, and everywhere is foot-marked in a tell-tale way. This gnarly old sour gum-tree has an opossum sleeping soundly among its roots, and the creature's curiosity in looking out in the night to judge of the weather has been re corded. You might not have noticed this, but some eyes are keener than others, and a hunter would have marked the spot. It seems that not every chestnut burr was opened and fell to the ground months ago. Here is one that has been dropped since the snow fell, and yet no chestnut-tree is very near. Squirrels again, and somewhere there is a hoard of food ; but no, burrs are not gathered, and the animals have found this burr lodged among the branches and tossed it down in play. After a snow-storm, if there has been no wind, whatsoever lies upon it comes there through some animal's intervention.

As to every tree in the woods, it is desirable to look at it from all points of view to learn all it has to tell you. To look up only is to see the under side of every branch, but what of the upper side ? Resting there may be some in- teresting creature peeping shyly over the edge and watching you. If you climb to the tops of trees and look down, the woods will tell you quite another story. The chances are you cannot do this, but do not say a tree or any cluster of them has little or nothing to tell until you have done so.   The silent man is not necessarily he who has least to say.

I have said that when the sun shone it was almost summery above our heads, if not about our feet.   Many a bird finds it so, and as every sound comes to you now peculiarly distinct, it is something worth the while to hear a bird sing, even to hear a passing snow-bird chirp, and, too, what endless amusement in that ceaseless comedy of the persecuting crows and the patient hawk ; an unused opportunity for some ornithological Shakespeare.   A word more of these unfailing friends of mine, the clamorous crows. "Occasionally," writes Lucretius, "the long-lived generations of crows . . . change their hoarse notes with the weather, when they are said (sometimes) to call for rain and showers and sometimes to cry for gales of wind."   Of a clear, sunny, midwinter day, as they pass over these woods or alight in the branches of the trees, they seem to be moved by pure joy in the fact of living, so rich, so content-full and eager is their every utterance.   I call my winter crows good company; friends that meet me half-way, and speak from their hearts; no mere mouthing of meaningless formalities. Then, as if to shame poor, shivering humanity that all too likely hugs the stove all day, a kinglet, almost our smallest bird, may come and chirp so cheerfully that you are moved to whistle in reply. Surely it is of some significance that shrews, our smallest mammals, and kinglets and winter wrens and the blessed chickadee, are as full of fun in January, with the mercury at zero, as ever a summer songster in the month of June.

Summer or winter, my love of trees is unalterable, ineradicable.

"The purple color of the murex so blends in one body with wool that it can never be extracted from it; not even if you should strive to restore the wool to its whiteness with all the waves of the sea; not even if the whole ocean, with all its floods, should be disposed to cleanse it."

Correspondents and Critics.

ON the last day of the year, unless plagued with the feeling that I have something better to do, I clear the cavernous pigeon-holes of my desk of the letters that have, for a twelve-month, been accumulating. It is not an altogether amusing way of passing an hour. A good many annoying thoughts return, for not every correspondent is reasonable or critic fair. I never have called back a dead year with un-mixed satisfaction; the sky is only clear in places, and ghosts of many clouds, some very black indeed, float by, with all the distinctness of the actual happening. But, in the long run, I feel as if a load was lifted from my shoulders when, having seen the accumulation of letters turned to ashes, I take a brisk walk over the meadows and return to my empty desk. I return, remembering, "You shall have time to wrangle in when you have nothing else to do," and the new year comes swiftly, as I determine to "cease to lament for that thou canst not help, and study help for that which thou lament'st."

Indulging, this New Year's eve, in retrospection before putting good resolutions to a practical test, I have thought that it is not an unmixed blessing that postage is so cheap. In that far-off day when to send a letter, if prepaid, meant an expenditure of twenty-five cents, most people thought twice or thrice before sitting down to announce that they took their pens in hand, and the world was happy then : perhaps happy as now. Many people were forced, because of the expense, to keep themselves unto themselves, and I would that this were now more true of them. We cannot limit our correspondents as we can our acquaintances, and I have occasionally wondered, with, I think, good reason, why I am singled out as the victim of queer correspondents, as they appear to me. Never intentionally have I forced myself upon any stranger's attention, but strangers have found me out, and an occasional remarkable letter is the result. Why I keep these communications, I do not know. Why I answered any of them is beyond explanation, but before burning the accumulation of the year I have been reading each one anew ; a contradictory procedure perhaps, but who is consistent among us ? I should add that my queer correspondents have found me out wholly because there have been publishers venturesome enough to print certain manuscripts of mine. This was a matter that concerned only the publishers, but it has been made the concern of other people also, especially the writers of certain letters, to which I have referred. A book is public property, but does the author also become public in the same sense ? My correspondents are mostly women. Why are they so inquisitive ? I once asked, and have since regretted my indiscretion. One prominent American authoress assures me man is nothing if not curious. His happiness consists in asking questions. He verges on insanity if he is not satisfied, and his persistence is in proportion to the matter in question being none of his business. I stand corrected and very humble, but puzzled too, when I remember that nearly all of my queer correspondents are women.

Let me particularize.   Seven of my correspondents have inquired anxiously about my
religion.   Now, I take it that if there is one
subject above another that is a purely personal
matter, it is a man's way of thinking on religious subjects.   Much as he may delight in
hearing sermons or following the intricacies of
more or less elaborate rituals, and generally as
he may approve of this, that, or the other sect,
he is, if truly religious, a law unto himself, and
if he is astray and ultimately misses heaven, it
is his loss and not a reflection on his more fortunate neighbors.   It is scarcely going too far
to say, if any one sees fit to ignore the whole
subject and take the chances, it is not the business of his neighbors to interfere.   I write this
without a trace of impatience or ill nature.   The
world thinks otherwise.   I took the trouble once
to say what I have just written, and what a raking
over the coals was the result!   My correspondent claimed to have "a call" to change the
current of my thoughts and turn me into an
unfamiliar path, and her peace of mind was
only acquired by a second communication, still
insisting I was religiously incorrect.   Particularly

do the Friends find fault with me, which is most strange of all. I would an honest jury could try the case, for I think I am more a Foxite than foxy. It is humiliating to think that, having lived for more than half a century in a Quaker atmosphere, I am still a stranger in a strange land.

Next is a little packet of five letters, all of which are devoted to the subject of tobacco. Do I use it in any form? One woman anticipates my reply by hoping I will not indulge in platitudes on use and abuse of the vile weed, saying, "no one can use it without its abusing the user." It is idle to combat fanaticism. It is best defeated by allowing it to work out its own destruction. "Thee admits being a smoker, so I cannot purchase another of thy books." This seems incredible, but it is true; and I wonder how many readers would be lost by a tirade against tobacco. Seriously, does the smoke from my cigar travel indefinitely far and offend the nostrils of an unknown correspondent? Why should my example for evil be more potent than that of the individual who finds, or fails to find, his livelihood in other lines of activity? I have never advised budding manhood to commence the use of tobacco, and would banish cigarettes from the world,—perhaps fanaticism on my part,—but it is simply silly for well-intentioned fanatics to ask grown men to cease to do that which does them no harm because youth may follow in their footsteps on reaching years of discretion. I feel that I am venturing a little too far, am treading on treacherous ground and calling down vengeance on my head when I suggest that a little too much stress is put upon this matter of exposure to temptation. Any youth of any intellect worthy the name knows that he is playing with fire when he reaches the age at which the so-called temptations become such to him, and downfall means full often merely a weak intellect, for however "brainy" a man may be, he is intellectually weak if he cannot draw the line between use and abuse. My feeling is, that while it may be very noble to be self-sacrificing, the fact has not been established that the world has evolved in this direction. It may turn to such a channel, but before it does I must continue to offend some queer correspondents by indulging in an occasional good cigar.

It is a much more difficult matter to comment, without loss of temper, upon the thirteen letters received concerning rum. Here again, as in the use of tobacco, it seems to me that the writers of these letters had better have spent their energies among people nearer their own homes, and let me, an unoffending stranger, alone. Certainly my opinion on the subject of the use of wine is absolutely of no importance. Because I have wandered by the brookside watching little fishes or listening to little birds in the bushes above the water, is apparently no reason why strangers should be curious as to what appears upon my table. These same people do not question their butcher and baker, but swallow their wares without comment, but hesitate to swallow mine until assured there is no alcohol in my drink. I will not say of all this that it matters nothing, for it does. It shows that fanaticism can, like ambition, overleap itself. The author of a book is not, more than another, his brother's keeper, and the would-be reader who wishes to know in advance whether or not I use wine is a reader not worth having. I have never felt it a duty to devote a page or two, now and then, to temperance! My critical correspondents should first wait until I have advocated some practice objectionable to them before assuming what is my attitude towards it, and commenting thereupon.

"What stand hast thou taken with reference to liquor? I fear thee does not look upon it with unalterable disapproval, from a remark in one of thy books." Here is an instance of a solid shot sent point-blank into my unsuspecting self. The page or chapter is not given, so I know not where to look, and would not take the trouble if I did. I do not make a practice of asking people for advice or information, if I can get the former through experience or the latter from the encyclopædia, but here is something different. I would that some one would tell me, and give me logical reasons, why I should forego my glass of currant wine on Christmas eve, to which I have been accustomed from my youth up. That glass never led me to empty the bottle any more than the accompanying bit of fruit-cake led to the demolition, by me, of the whole loaf. I note that my correspondent is a Friend, and I further note that

not all Friends have yet ceased to make currant wine, nor do they manipulate it in such a
way that it is non-alcoholic.

When the first ciderless mince-pie came upon
a certain farmer's table, the good man remarked,
"Martha, thee has certainly made some mistake. I will take a piece of the pumpkin."
As I view it, Martha had made a very big mistake, and so do some of my correspondents.

But let us to a more cheerful subject. Here
is a pile of begging letters that reached me
soon after the appearance of a little book. The
impression seems to be in every case that an
"author's copy" costs nothing. That happy
individual has but to direct the sending of the
volume to So-and-So, and there the matter ends.
One correspondent, an Indiana schoolmistress,
tells me as much, and her letter in particular is
worthy of a moment's consideration. She in-
forms me that she does not suppose my copy-
right interest is more than ten per cent., and
so the book was only worth fifteen cents to me,
and she did not think that too much to ask for.
Where under the sun, as thus viewed, does the
publisher come in? I asked her as much,

promising the book on receipt of a satisfactory reply, for which, I will add, I am still waiting. Publishers cannot say henceforth that I have not been duly alive to their interests. So far as I am aware, merchants are not plagued with letters asking a gift of the wares in which they deal. Schoolmistresses, even, do not beg, but buy their candy and clothing, so why not the books they desire? To single out the product of an author's brain from all other material things as objects not coming under commercial considerations is, from the author's point of view, inexplicable. It is sadly true there is precious little money in the average book, but then, just so much the more reason for the author wishing to receive the whole of that little. I do not know if publishers are as pestered as are authors in this way; probably not; and certainly the former are not sentimental to the point of startling generosity unless some how or way they are roundly well paid for it. May the Indiana schoolmistress never see my concluding sentence : what wonderful people do we have in this world, truly !

One letter—from a man this time—asks me

how I interpret Nature, and goes on to say he cannot for the life of him see very much when he takes a walk. "I know a tree's a tree and a rock's a rock, but then I'm stuck." He is not one whit more stuck than I am in trying to reply. I have been trying for six months to formulate some sort of answer and have only gotten so far as " Dear Sir." "The Interpretation of Nature" is a very pretty title for an essay, but who dare tackle it? Thoreau might have done so, but our home fields have been left without a master-hand since his day.

I have nothing to say upon the art of interpreting Nature, for that is really what my correspondent means, but here are thoughts that I have had upon the subject; disjointed thinking, as I rambled all too aimlessly down the wood-path and over the ever-suggestive meadows. I cull these brevities from many note-books, picking here and there among the many mentionings of bird and beast and flower.

Life is short at best, and to no one is given intellectual range to cover the whole field of knowledge. We are necessarily dependent upon others for the greater part of what we acquire in the way of information, and how disheartening to find a cherished fact gathered from one source asserted to be but a fancy in another. What are we to believe? This is a gloomy question that dogs our steps, harries our nerves, and proves hopelessly confusing from early manhood to life's close.

The interpretation of Nature! She yet needs to be interpreted in many directions and the cloud lifted that still renders misty what should be clear as noonday. It is true, as bright raindrops come from murky clouds, so crystal clear facts are born of doubt and wrangling, but is such a birth a necessity? Nature does not withhold the truth, but into what strange vessels do the precious facts occasionally fall! Vessels that have some malign power by which the plain is rendered obscure; the clear made murky; the direct and straight made aimless and crooked. He is the exception, we are almost led to think, who can carry from the laboratory to the world at large a newly acquired fact without marring its beauty or befogging its significance. Can it be that the remedy lies within ourselves? This is much like making every one the superior of his neighbor in his own estimation, and leads to what is thoroughly to be deplored, a very low estimate of our neighbor's capabilities. On the other hand, too great confidence in our own powers as surely leads to so grave an error as to underestimate the strength of others. We have need to be very humble when self-measurement is called for, but do not let the pendulum swing too far in the other direction. I long ago elected myself the entire faculty of a college whereat my own conscience is the only student. Success calls for rational confidence in our own powers, and the development of these powers must not be left wholly with others. We should be reasonably ambitious to express our own views, and not merely reflect the impressions and beliefs of others. We need not cultivate incredulity, but a statement being made, verify it where possible rather than blindly accept, and particularly is this called for in the inter-pretation of Nature's near-at-hand and readily approached phenomena. We cannot all own telescopes, and must accept our astronomy from the fortunate few who nightly read the starry skies and trace the comet's course ; but we can own microscopes and use unaided eyes to our own advantage ; correcting, it may be, others' errors and adding not only to our own stock of knowledge but to that of the world's.   Do not, as is so often the case, believe that it is always your neighbor and never yourself whom Nature selects as her interpreter.   Do not, above all things, tremble in the presence of learned greatness, but ask yourself how it comes that they know so much and you so little.   Solve that problem and you have bridged the yawning chasm between you.

There is no career for man, or none worth following, that does not bring him into more or less close contact with Nature, so why all your life a stranger to her?   Your indifference will not yield you any extra dollars.   Ignorance may be lucky at times, but in the long run knowledge comes out ahead.   Why, for instance, be not as weather-wise as your neighbor? If the wind or clouds can be read, why not read for yourself and not listen to another?   One newspaper would not meet the needs of a village even, yet one naturalist is not to be found among ten thousand men.   Even if mere transient pleasures is our life's aim, do we attain to the fulness thereof shut up within our little selves? We need not fear that we shall lose our precious selves because we wander in thought beyond the shadows of our door-yard trees. I pity those who look with admiration at the bird's-eye maple or wrinkled oak that make the sideboard and see in them only a pretty background for sparkling glass and glittering silver: see this only, and are never carried in imagination or actually go to the forest where the oak and maple grow. How frequently the soul of honesty robs itself! How generally, I fancy, women would cease to be murderers if they traced back the history of the plumes in their hats! Is what Nature vouchsafes them of so poor a quality, unattractive or repulsive, that the skin of a bird is called for as an offset to their ugliness? Woman may think so, but her plainness is only the more apparent when crowned with an evidence of heartlessness. Be she ever so careful, no housekeeper can prevent animal life from crossing the door-sill or darting through an open window. Around the evening lamp curiously marked moths will flutter at

times, and usually only call forth mild execra-
tion, as they annoy us, while reading. Have
you frequently, indeed, ever, met with the man
or woman who laid aside newspaper or embroid-
ery for a time to see how many species were
to be gathered by merely extending an arm? I
never met with such a one save once ; yet it is
an incontrovertible fact that no more profitable
evening can be spent than in an artless way
studying the entomology of the library table.
No one is so free of the earth, earthy, as not to
"cuss" a mosquito, but how often are they intelligently discussed?

It is not an exaggeration to say that conster-
nation fills the room if a spider drops from the
ceiling, and through fear the room is emptied
if a mouse runs from a corner. Had we, even
if ever so little, interpreted Nature or even
tried to do so and failed, would not such exhibitions of our silliness be impossible? We
read in the daily papers—too often vehicles of
distorted facts—harrowing accounts of blood-
poisoning following bites of mice, spiders, and
even the scratch of kitty's claws, but what are
the chances really of being bitten by a mouse

or spider, or scratched by a cat; perhaps one in a million, and not one in a million bites are poisonous. Too, if we were more disposed to attend to Nature we would lessen our susceptibility to blood-poisoning. Clear your brain and your blood will take care of itself.

"But Nature is so uninteresting," exclaims some one in your hearing. When we meet with uninteresting people, we generally remember them as such and avoid frequent meetings in the future; but these uninteresting people have some sense and do not force themselves into your presence. Nature never intrudes,—please remember that, ye devotees of artificiality. Nature is all too often uninteresting, and why? Because we are taught to turn our backs upon her at the very outsets of our careers. The curious child, attracted by a gaudy caterpillar, stops in its play to admire the creature creeping before him and is suddenly and violently snatched away by the fool of a nurse, who assures the disappointed and now bewildered child that the caterpillar will bite or sting. A lie is crammed down the child's throat, and it will be years before the mischief done in a moment can be repaired. I have put this upon the ignorant nurse, but the supposedly well educated parents are not one whit better. Educated! Yes, by courtesy, we say so, but what a deviation from the exact state of affairs! Can any one be considered educated who has absolutely no knowledge of Nature? To daily handle objects and yet know nothing of their origin, to know a brick and never to have heard of clay, is not to be worthily educated. If a child's mind is led in the right direction at the very start and inquisitiveness, which is natural, is judiciously encouraged rather than savagely repressed, there will be obviated the great defect now so prominent, when we survey the minds of the masses, indifference as to Nature. Strangely enough, in later years, the mistake of neglecting natural knowledge is recognized by many, and yet no pains are taken to prevent the children from undergoing their own sad experiences. This is culpable. To see a child taught a downright lie and not lift a finger to prevent it occurs every day, yet the bystander knows that the child will suffer as he or she has done. There never was a child of sound mind that was not at one time a naturalist, and how far this tendency of the intellect is to be encouraged is a question of importance. Not every one can be a professional zoologist and devote a lifetime thereto to the exclusion of all else, but interest in such subjects should never be chilled. As such matters are now regulated, we find a silly mother afraid of a mouse, and the child must run no imaginary dangers. The very mention of snakes blanches many a cheek, yet probably not one dangerous snake is within miles of the speaker. Disadvantageous prejudice is inherited, has been since the days of distant ancestry, and we make no effort to look coolly at the facts and endeavor to uproot the silly whims that have such a clutch upon us. When our remote ancestry lived in trees and were in positive danger from the attacks of poisonous serpents, a fear of snakes was rational. That was the origin of the mental status that still enthralls the majority of the people we meet, but is it rational to let an impression like this go unstudied for some hundred thousand years ! It is not true that snakes chase people. If the two happen to take the same direction, there is no evidence of one pursuing and the other being pursued. If the frightened man will stop, the snake will keep straight on, and the conditions reversed, the man continuing his course will pursue the snake. The present great art of lying would be one of the minor accomplishments if there had been no snakes in the world. Fish have never damaged man's veracity like the poor, much maligned serpents. Is there, then, no good reason for rational interpretation of Nature?

The secret of successful interpretation is very largely the determination of the inter-relation of phenomena. Isolated facts are merely parts of a great whole, the recognition of which constitutes knowledge. The mere gathering of dissociated facts has been so long considered the acquiring of an education, it is not to be wondered at that we have so many learned ignoramuses among us. Bald statements but emphasize our ignorance. The robin builds a mud-lined nest, the oriole a pendent one, the bank-swallow burrows in the cliff; why? What is our mere statement but evidence that we have taken the first step and could not or will not take a second?   Occasionally we have evidence in a volume that many steps have been taken, as in "Origin of Species," but how generally are the books set before us but bundles of finger-posts, and these not always set in the right directions!   To tell yourself or another that frogs leap and snakes creep is to publish yourself as yet in an infant class, if you cannot back your assertion with at least the mechanics of leaping and creeping.   If your own desire leads no farther than the witnessing of the act, you can never hope to be a naturalist.   Strange indeed are some of the entries made in note-books.   A list of forty birds seen in one day is now lying before me, with not one word of comment concerning a single specimen.   Better to have spent the whole day with an English sparrow.   "It is a contribution to geographical distribution," says one.   "The date shows that these birds are summer residents, if not all-the-year-round birds," says another.   "Forty birds seen and nothing more," I reply.   As to geographical distribution, it has been done to death, and always will be, seeing it is easy and the list-makers outnumber observers in a wide sense;

and as to our birds, the subject can never be forever set at rest, seeing that the birds will not obey the rules, and only laugh at notices to effect that this field belongs to another species : No trespassing.   Unfortunately, birds are the arch-trespassers of wild life.   There is no barrier that they cannot surmount if they choose to do so ; no solid sheets of air, like plate-glass partitions, through which they cannot go.   That they do not overstep far more than they do is to be wondered at, and that geographical distribution is so much of a factor of our ornithology is strange, seeing that some of our weaker-winged birds travel north and south for an enormous distance twice a year.   That faunal lines can be drawn where there are no mountain ranges even to be crossed is a remarkable feature of this subject as applied to my own neighborhood.   A man can walk from Maine to Florida ; any bird can fly that distance.   Some do so ; why not all ?   Perhaps, why do any ?   We have not yet solved the problem of migration, and now the question rises, Has it varied since the earlier records of the phenomenon ?   We know that some birds have left us that were once abundant, the crane, pelican, and even some inland song-birds, as the mocker and summer tanager. Why? Better determine this than kill the innocents to measure the curve of their toe-nails. Given a real problem, we shrink from the undertaking and fall back upon egg-measurements. In one direction migration has changed, it is losing its regularity, and we are blessed with longer visits from some migrants, and others are plucky as ourselves and face the winter with even better grace. I would like to grow enthusiastic over winter catbirds and chewinks at Christmas, but they have as yet developed no peculiarities over these same birds of summer. They find more berries than insects, but the latter are not wholly wanting. There is never a day when loose leaves and unfrozen ground are not to be found, and here there are creeping things in numbers, if not innumerable. I did think that the winter catbird lived exclusively on the berries of our greenbrier; now I know better. He hobnobs gracefully with chewinks, and they toss over the dead leaves in company, dividing the spoils and never thinking of quarrelling. No birds are less associated in summer. So warm are many nooks and sheltered ravines that the Maryland yellow-throat forgets to consult the almanac, and seems to mistake November's Indian summer for September sunshine. Not always, not often, but then not rarely. Will it become a fixed habit in time? It is such with the catbird, the chewink, and to less extent the brown thrasher. They can almost always be found in the pine woods or dense oak-growths curtained with usnea ; places where they are not apt to be in summer. Are these pointers in the direction of migratorial change of habit? And what of the southward flight of swallows of several species that occurs in November, weeks after our residents have taken their departure. This occurs two, perhaps three, years in every five. These are matters that any one can study, and the untrained observer is as well fitted to the task as many a theory-crushed professional ornithologist. The facts gathered, the little attendant circumstances that may mean so much, are less likely to be overlooked by those curious as to such matters and who have not their senses taken away because the birds are out of place, out of season, playing hookey instead of being at school. Knowledge is retarded by calling an over-staying bird a "straggler," as it is learnedly pronounced to be. It is a pestiferous word that covers ignorance, like "malaria" so constantly upon the tongue of the physician when diagnosis is beyond his skill. The bald fact is, birds more and more are spending their winters far north of where they did some years ago, or else we are just finding out that the old observers were in error. The latter case is not probable, and now, recognizing a change, we are given an opportunity to test our skill in solving a problem. We are saved vain specu-lation as to influence exerted by a change of climate, because we have meteorological tabu-lations showing that no change has taken place thermometrically. It is just as cold now in January as when the pilgrims landed or, proba-bly, when the Norsemen sighted our shores, but there is a difference that may have its bearing upon the subject, we have less snow. Can it be that the absence of snow, making the finding of food more practicable, has its influence? It will doubtless be urged that the birds leave

long before the time for snow.   This would be
a weighty argument did the birds leave so early
in the autumn, but they do not.   My own
records, covering many years, go to show that
over-staying birds have been observed most
frequently when the ground was bare, and on
many occasions when the weather was about as
cold as at any time during the winter.   Promptly
on the occurrence of a snow-storm these birds
disappear.   I can never find them, but when
the snow is melted they return.   Where are
they in the mean time?   People who do not
hourly consult the thermometer are unaware to
a great extent of the ups and downs of the
mercury, and birds having no such contrivance
are equally ignorant of the proximity, at times,
to zero of the sensitive metal.   Judging from
their actions, at least, we are logically led to
presume so.   Whether birds feel the cold or the
extreme heat is altogether another matter.   It
is whether or not they are influenced by it.
Finding it less formidable than they supposed,
they have stayed occasionally, years ago, and
one after another has followed the example set
until now it is not unusual.   But was this over-

staying habit spread by example?   It may seem a childish question to ask, but what of direct communication of ideas?   Here, certainly, Nature has not been exhaustively interpreted.   I am not aware that any number of ornithologists have studied bird-language as something separate and apart from bird-song.   Does it exist? How are we to determine?   I have long been familiar with a man who has lived all his days within sight and hearing of crows.   He claims to understand their language and can repeat the "words" that make up their vocabulary.   Certainly, they seem to talk, but do they?   Does a certain sound made by them have a uniform significance?   Year after year I have listened and watched, watched and listened, and wondered if my friend was right.   He believes it.   I believe it.   Is an ultimate positive assurance a hopeless expectation?   Are there limitations to ornithological interpretation?   We know that crows are cunning, and by their mother wit have withstood the persecutions of mankind; we know that they have a wide range of utterances and not one is intended to merely gratify the ear, and yet we hesitate to say plainly that crow talketh unto crow and take counsel together. There is no reason why this should not be the case ; there is abundant evidence pointing in that direction, but no actual demonstration has taken place. Probably none can be had, and we must be content with inferential interpretation. This is not as useless as has been claimed, and is readily set aside when a mathematical demonstration is forthcoming. Long association with living birds results in acquiring impressions that are far worthier of credence than the theories of holiday excursionist birdmen ; and the insulting charge of "investing birds with imaginary attributes" is silly beyond comparison, but not surprising considering its source. The farmer that has had to battle with crows and purple grackles and outwit the cunning of a pigeon-hawk has interpreted these birds' mental status with a higher average of correctness than any professional ornithologist possibly could do. The farmer reaches the goal of reasonable recognition without having any such intention ; he is taught without a desire to be informed, and with freedom from theoretical bias comes proportionate certainty. He is convinced long before the ornithologist comes to a definite conclusion. When there is agreement, the question is settled forever; when a divergence, the element of probability lies in the farmer's direction. The birds about a farm-house door-yard are not always the birds in the books, and for one I prefer the former and what they have to teach us. The bittern that goes fishing, at Christmas, in the open water of the home meadow is more interesting to me than those of its kind that seek their comfort in far southern swamps. I love a bird at all times, but none more dearly than the myrtle warbler, that chirps in its own cheerful way as it threads the tangled tree-tops when winter winds are blowing; and when the Carolina wren comes to my window and shouts its joy, though a storm be raging, I cease to work and listen.

But the world is not merely a big bird-cage. What is the meaning of the meadow-mouse that leaps away, bounding like a kangaroo, yet with no exaggerated hind legs like that animal? Why does it not run merely and keep hidden in the weeds? Here is a chance to get a closer view of the workings of Nature than the scalpel alone will lead you to. Indeed, the action contradicts the knife ; the mouse doing that which it has not, in one sense, the ability to do, or not the facilities wherewith to do it. It has an emergency to meet, and must we cover up our ignorance by prattle about instinct? These mice are everywhere in the meadows, and not a punky log in the marsh but has been tunnelled by them and made a snug harbor against attacks from enemies, and he is rash who claims full knowledge of all the dangers to which they are subjected. We have stopped short in our investigations of the habits of our most familiar forms of wild life, and continually forget that the constantly changing surroundings must have some effect upon an animal's mentality. Less closely observed, mammals have given rise to some wrong impressions, and the untechnical observer is irritating because of his obstinacy. Many farmers insist, and probably always will, that our common mole eats sweet potatoes and the seed of watermelons that have so often to be replanted. Appearances are against the moles, for they do go through the very spots where the seeds and plants are placed, and how generally, from man to the mole, does condemnation descend with unpitying severity, and the truth never regarded, even though trumpet-tongued! Ignorant farmer, in this case; but let the learned mammalogist be very sure that he has never blundered.

To return to the meadow-mouse. By merest chance I got what I think is an inkling of why it jumps; or is it a case of misinterpreted appearances? There was a full-grown garter-snake in pursuit. Did the mouse keep closely to the ground and depend upon running only it would prove a short chase, but when the pursued creature leaps above the grass, now in one direction, now in another, the snake is bewildered, and the mouse gains sufficient headway to reach some safely sheltering spot. Of course the mouse would soon become exhausted and the snake ultimately overtake it. So, at least, I interpreted what I had witnessed. Possibly many another explanation might be brought forward, but I am satisfied with my own effort to make clear the purpose of the mouse I watched, and do not obstruct the ultimate acquisition of the truth so long as I am willing to be set right where unquestionably wrong. We can have abundant faith in ourselves without losing faith in others, and we wrong ourselves when we let others lead us wheresoever we go, as if blind from birth. Our eyes and ears were not intended solely for a few purely personal considerations. We dwarf our powers when we survey a parlor or a kitchen but never the landscape, as we do, also, when we discourse learnedly over the merits, as food, of Delaware shad or trout of the mountain brook, yet never see a silvery minnow in the muddy mill-pond. There is not a person living, perhaps, who will not claim to know a minnow when he sees it, but you will look in vain through the entire range of ichthyological literature for information as to just when and where these same little minnows lay their eggs. We are as ignorant to-day of the habits of our most widely spread species as was the Delaware Valley's palæolithic man of X-rays.

Thoreau records that he felt better acquainted with a pretty purple grass when he learned its scientific name. Before then it stood aloof; something separate and apart from the surrounding objects seen in his daily walks; but learning the names of strangers, do we know enough? So far as humanity is concerned, often it is enough, you will say; but so unfortunate a feeling should not apply to the wild life about us. Not a creature that we see but serves some purpose, but if we are asked what that purpose is, the chances are against our ability to make a worthy reply. Man is not only in the world, but of it. He proudly claims to know his own place; but he is best informed who knows not only where he himself belongs, but where every bird that flies, fish that swims, and creeping creature crawls also belongs. He that knows this sees with a clearer eye, hears with a quicker ear, and walks with a steadier gait; from his youth, upward and onward, to the end.

Critics! One of them stands forth for professional inerrancy and says he has no quarrel with amateurs. As the latter are everywhere a vast concourse to one, what if the army of amateurs proclaim their indifference to this self-conscious professional, who can be tripped on many a page? The fatal mistake of the pro-

fessional is that the life-long amateur has necessarily spent his days in vain ; that he has merely
tickled his fancy and pleased himself during
leisure hours, but never gained much knowledge or acquired skill ; in short, merely hovered
about the skirts of the omniscient professional,
ever looking at the unattainable with longing
eyes and ultimately dying in despair. This, I
say, is the view of the professional, and just so
far as it is true the professional is apt to make
himself ridiculous. There are men learned in
the law who are not lawyers ; men who are
deeply versed in theological discussion, yet are
neither bishop, priest, nor deacon ; men who
know more than the rudiments of medicine,
though this matters not, seeing every man is
a fool or physician at forty, yet lay no claim
to M.D. after their names. So, too, it is in
the study of Nature. There are many men,
amateurs or lovers, let us say, of birds, that are
better authorities, so far as their own neighborhoods are concerned, than the petulant professional who calmly announces that he has no
quarrel with amateurs. Who under the broad
canopy of heaven cares if he has ? What the

world wants is familiarity with the life about it; an intelligent knowledge of beast, bird, and insect, and this is sometimes, yes, often, to be had from the pages of amateurs, or literally, lovers or enthusiasts of the subjects treated, rather than from the technical pages of the professional. Certainly it cannot be said that the knowledge of the latter is necessarily accurate, or why should these self-elected wiseacres differ so among themselves? The earnest amateur has as clear vision, as acute ears, and as critical a mind as any professional that ever lived. An artist, on having his attention called to a brilliant sunset, exclaimed, impatiently, that the colors were ill arranged; a musician, on being asked his opinion of the sunset song of a thrush, replied that the discord jarred upon his nerves; so the professional ornithologist seeing a bird out of place, nesting out of time, or singing when it was expected to be silent, shrugs his shoulders and mutters, "It is not recorded so in any book." Happy amateurs! that are moved to take Nature as they find it and see beauty in the sunset sky, hear melody in the wild-bird's song, and only wish they too had been equally fortunate when their fellows find roses in January and ice in June. To the world at large, I fancy, this enthusiasm of amateurs is ever as welcome and not less instructive than the technicalities of the professional.

But it has been claimed with much argument, if not always with logic, that critics should never be criticised. That, in other words, they were a privileged class to whom was allotted the privilege of saying what they chose, but must not be answered; their decisions borne in meekness. It may be very foolish, when called a name, to call back, but sometimes to do so abounds in deep satisfaction.

If there was no more life and suggestiveness in the bird-world than is recorded in the recent hand-books, outlines and nondescript dilutions of ornithology, then the new Audubon societies have no cause for organization; the birds are of no use that warrant their protection. Song-birds that do not sing, and all birds that cut no capers and have too little soul to animate their feathers, would never draw us out of our houses to know what happens in the field or forest. To know the anatomy of birds down to the remotest details is most desirable, but this is the beginning, not the end, of knowledge ; a fact that the professional perpetually forgets. A man may have an astonishing knowledge of men yet know nothing of human anatomy ; and so, too, the amateur may know exhaustively the birds that throng his path from year to year, yet not the number of feathers in their tails or whether they are more properly classified in section C than D of Grand Division A or B. That knowledge that comes to us directly from the field, through eyes and ears, has a value equal to any we can derive from books, even though professionals have written them.

A serious error on the part of the proud professional is his contemptuous reception or ill-mannered rejection of information offered by the native of some backwoods region as to the fauna and flora of the locality. As if all the books and museums together could be pitted against the life-long experience of those to the *manor* born. It signifies nothing that the professional can show the native no end of objects that he never saw before and can make plain what previously was a profound mystery. That is but one side of the question ; for the native, if of ordinary wit, can upset the professional's preconceptions of geographical distribution and asserted mathematical regularity of habit. It is not wise to tell the native that this or that creature is not to be found, or that it is here now but not then, and all such rubbish. When I heard, years ago, that mighty hunter, Tin-cup Tommy, told that there was not an otter in all Crosswicks Creek, I happened to catch a strange glitter in his eye and overheard the scarcely breathed oath that accompanied his comments. Well, Tin-cup Tommy sold two otter-skins that winter, and he trapped both animals in Crosswicks Creek. When a learned naturalist, some years later, said in his hearing that English snipe never nested here, he pinched my arm in a very meaningful manner, and brought nest, eggs, and old birds to town to prove that they did, and he was not again contradicted in that quarter. When asked if barn-owls were common, he said he could bring, if wanted, a basketfull of " monkey faces," and did. I wish I dare put upon the printed page his own words, good round oaths and all, when he asked me,

"What's the matter, anyhow, with them fellers from town. They know a heap, but somehow they've missed knowin' it all." That is the whole matter in a nutshell. They miss knowing it all, and he who would be so far accomplished—no one ever can be—or approach it, must give his life as practically to the subject as did my old friend Tommy. He was as much a feature of the meadows as any mink or muskrat; ay, as any minnow in the creek.

It is all very well for the closet student of anatomy and bibliography and the learned advocates of trinomial nomenclature to pose as the guardians of our inferior, amateurish intellects, but they should always remember that they do so by their own appointment, and not feel aggrieved if they are occasionally overlooked, or even asked to stand aside. It is not the geologist who finds the lump of gold, but the fellow with pick and shovel; the geologist comes later, to tell us how it all came about.

The professional, unfortunately for himself, becomes too theoretical, and, having devised a system, sees through ill-adjusted spectacles. Every straight line is crooked, every crooked one endlessly angular. He would have the wild life of the universe as obedient to him as the tyrant of a school-teacher has or would have the trembling scholars, but, alas! wild life will not be obedient. The poor fellow who was all upset when he first heard of a batrachian chorus in November would have gone into spasms, probably, had he walked over my meadows on December 17, 1897, when the air trembled with the croakings of ten thousand frogs. I do not know what would be his explanation of a barn-owl nesting in October, but not an old gunner hereabouts but knows that more than one kind of owl, that live all the year round in some hollow tree,—a fixture as much as a man that lives in his own house,—is not at all regular in its breeding, and young with down and "hair" have been seen in winter. The amateur does not know who is to blame, but snow will fall in April, covering the ground and drifting as beautifully as ever in January. Very odd to the people who dwell in town, but very commonplace to the unprofessional rustic. After all, it is not strange. Too little attention, for all these years, has been given to the fact that as the surface of the earth was rapidly changing, forests turned to treeless fields, swamps turned to dry pastures, streams obliterated or directed into artificial channels, Nature's handiwork, in short, swept out of existence; so, if wild life was to stay at all, it must face the problem of a changed surrounding and alter its ways of living accordingly. The fact that the frog's epithalamium is a characteristic feature of spring is no reason for supposing that the creature must necessarily be mute as an oyster at all other times; but to say so seemed so pretty a statement when originally made by some closet naturalist, that down into the books it went and there it stays. I do not know how long a flying-squirrel lives, but there has been a colony of them in the attic of my house for more than half a century. Those now living over my head, and that turn night into day, are as much creatures of the house as any mouse in the wall. It is true they go abroad more and have not lost their flight power, but I am sure they would feel strangely enough if suddenly taken to a forest and found themselves with no such shelter as my house affords. They have learned to recognize a human being; not to the extent of being dangerously trusty, but not frightened out of their wits when they meet me face to face.

Too much has been inferred from a limited range of observation ; but this is no excuse for the silly contradictions on the part of professionals to the assertions of amateurs. My green herons are not solitary, but distinctly social ; my wood-ducks do breed regularly and abundantly near here and have always done so. The English snipe nests in these meadows nearly every summer. King-rails are abundant in the mucky meadow, and so a long chapter could be, but need not be, written about such matters. My earnest advice to amateurs is to depend upon their own powers and turn a deaf ear to professionals, except where technicalities are required. Not that the professional is uninformed, but in proportion as you depend upon him you lose confidence in yourself. Rather be a law unto yourself and only unto yourself. Place your own ability in the highest place and look down, not up. The professional, remember, never invites you to be other than his slave ;

but so train your own self that you can dare to make of the professional a servant and not a master.

The professional has his place, and a pre-eminently prominent one it is ; so prominent and elevated indeed, that from the exalted height the level plains of the amateur's world are not seen distinctly. Bewildered and be-dizzied, the professional mars not makes for dignity by over-estimation of himself. His great good fortune in reaching professional rank proves occasionally too great and sober-ness is over-balanced. Why he so lauds him-self and smiles with a pitying glance on the modest amateur is not readily explained. It does not decrease the amateur's value, and cer-tainly does not add height or depth or breadth to professional erudition. The professor of ornithology can issue no edict forever ending ornithic irregularities ; cat-bird, heron, snipe, thrush, and owl will do precisely as they please. Grasshoppers will caper over the snow, eels wander overland, and catfish brave the air upon occasion. Opossums will walk the streets of a town, raccoons hide in cellars, and weasels attack men ; a thousand things occur that are in the line of unusual occurrence, but not so unusual as some would have us believe. It is but an exhibition of ignorance to call anything not in the line of supposed habits an "accidental occurrence," and so of no significance. How do these offensively bumptious professionals know that it is "accidental"? Have they been for years so much abroad, or does every "accidental occurrence" flatly contradict the known course of any creature's life? The amateur will ever do himself a service in turning a deaf ear to these snap judgments of professionals. Every unusual happening is an added fact for the amateur of which he can make good use. The amateur can be happy, and wisely so, with his few facts or many as the case may be ; but no professional, be he ever so wise, but has yet something more to learn. His will not be a well-rounded and worthy career until he learns to look with respect upon amateurs and what they know and do, for all too likely are the chances that from them his incomplete professional knowledge might receive a few finishing touches that lacking, leaves him, at last, standing before the world an unfinished monument to erudition.

An amusing feature of this matter is the question of veracity. Now, I speak soberly when I say that the most recklessly inexact man I ever met is a geologist. He no more considers facts that jostle his theories than he does the ground upon which he treads. To be sure, few people read geological essays, and surely none of his will find their way to text-books, so little mischief is done. Lackeys of government bureaus too often, to make sure of their salaries, are forced to keep their mouths shut or to lie! Now, any amateur, be he ever so careful, may prove to be mistaken. He may see one thing and believe it to be another; but the professional is treading on very thin ice when he flatly contradicts the amateur's statement; particularly when there is no impossibility entering into the case. Fight the amateur's statement as improbable by all means, but it is a dangerous thing to flatly contradict it,—dangerous, because when the amateur proves that he is correct these same professionals invariably decline to take back their offensive words, and righteously merit the occasional castigation they receive. Perhaps, though, all things considered, such attacks should not be considered offensive. I believe the amateur is wise in paying no attention to them. They reflect only upon those who make them, and the world gives little heed to such matters. The people ask for facts, not theories, when it is a question of natural history. A notable instance of this is in the recent off-hand dictum of a world-renowned archæologist who has never seen the valley of the Delaware unless from a car-window, but, accepting the assertions of an incompetent and reckless theorist, says that we have no evidence of man's antiquity hereabouts. I, who have lived here all my life, say that we have. The world is free to choose between us. It is just such instances as these that confuse the mind of the general public and sometimes dishearten amateurs, who have enthusiastically entered upon the investigation of what Nature has done, and is doing, in their own neighborhoods.

Not a syllable of comment on the savants of the day. There are many such, and never one

too many ; but these real students of any subject are students at heart always, and never turn
a deaf ear to the suggestions of some humble
thinker to whom Nature may have made a suggestion. Certainly, it is incumbent upon every
right thinking man to give every novel suggestion a respectful hearing. Ideas that were
stamped as absurd at their birth have survived
the unjust assaults and later revolutionized the
world of thought.

The dividing line between amateur and
professional has never been quite satisfactorily
drawn. Some sudden change in worldly cir-
cumstance may induce the amateur to make his
studies his life-work, and, Presto ! Change ! he
is from that moment professional ; and what a
change it sometimes proves to be ! Ashamed,
it would seem, of his former self, he actually
looks down upon amateurish work with disdain ;
yet an unbiassed observer cannot discover by
so much as the breadth of a hair how he of to-
day differs from him of yesterday.

The amateur naturalist has everything to be
thankful for and few reasons for serious sorrow.
Far removed from a controversial atmosphere,

it is his to breathe the unpolluted air of the field and forest ; to see and hear, to taste and smell and touch, yet never to be weighted with the doubts with which the wrangling professionals befog the pleasant landscape. Their knowledge may be untechnical, but so far as it extends it is not untrue, and that, and that only, is the worthy aim, the honorable ambition, of the honest amateur.

Index.

THE END.